"THERE SHE IS! SEIZE HER AT ONCE!"

Endril went for his knife, but the place was tightly packed and before he could draw, the squad of armored men had imprisoned Elizebith. Two officials in frilly costumes arrived. A drumroll began. "We summon the witchpricker!" A bent old man limped across the floor. He held up a nasty device resembling a dagger. "If this device shall pierce the breast of this woman causing no wound, she shall be proved a witch!"

Bith struggled and kicked to no avail. The old man stepped up to her and dramatically plunged the blade into her chest. . . .

The Runesword Series

OUTCASTS by Clayton Emery
SKRYLING'S BLADE by Rose Estes and Tom Wham

THE DREAMSTONE by J.F. Rivkin
(coming in March 1991)

Volume Two

SKRYLING'S BLADE

Rose Estes and Tom Wham

ACE BOOKS, NEW YORK

This book is an Ace original edition,
and has never been previously published.

SKRYLING'S BLADE

An Ace Book / published by arrangement with
Bill Fawcett & Associates

PRINTING HISTORY
Ace edition / November 1990

ISBN: 0-441-73695-5

Ace Books are published by The Berkley Publishing Group,
200 Madison Avenue, New York, New York 10016.
The name ''ACE'' and the ''A'' logo
are trademarks belonging to Charter Communications, Inc.

PRINTED IN THE UNITED STATES OF AMERICA

10 9 8 7 6 5 4 3 2 1

CHAPTER
1

The crackling fire had burned down to a bed of glowing red coals and the three figures seated at the table were nodding, nearly asleep. A fourth stood up quietly and slipped out of the room and into the cool night without making a sound. Moments later the innkeeper peeped in from the kitchen, and shook his head.

"When will they ever leave?" he mumbled to himself. The old man then shuffled out into the dining room and began cleaning up the dishes and mugs that were strewn about the tables.

The four heroes of Cairngorm had been more than welcome at first, and he had gladly offered them food and shelter for as long as they liked. They had driven back Schlein and the evil armies of the Dark Lord. As a result, the foul Mistwall, a strange cloud-like thing that was creeping relentlessly across the civilized world, had receded and now this was a happier land . . . . But these four had been here all winter, showing no sign of wanting to leave, and they were eating him out of house and home! However, thanks to them, at least he *had* a home. He sighed, and trudged back to the kitchen with a tray full of crockery, dropped it on the table with a crash, and then went upstairs to his room for the night.

Hathor jerked awake at the sound from the kitchen, and looked slowly around the room. The dim glow of the coals accented the red hair that topped his massive head. Though the light was dim, his troll night vision took in all. There was Bith, with her long dark hair flowing down over her soft shoulders, and the boy warrior, Cal, nodding at the table with his sharpening stone clutched to his breast. Endril was gone, as usual. The elf had made it a regular practice to disappear each night into the beech forests that surrounded the village.

A more unlikely group had never been assembled, thought the troll. They were all outcasts of sorts. He himself had left the dark caves and given up trollkind to live among the humans; Cal was an out-of-work soldier whose lord had mysteriously fled the battlefield, as well as the face of the earth; Endril no longer lived among the elves and refused further explanation, and strangest of all was Bith, the daughter of the powerful evil sorceress Morea. She had left the easy life in her mother's castle, now engulfed by the Mistwall, to wander on her own.

Hathor put his mug to his lips and swallowed the remaining quart of ale in one long gulp and then belched loudly. He reached over and shook Bith gently.

"Time to sleep," he said, softly.

The young princess stirred. "Oh . . . it's you, Thor." She yawned and stretched like a cat, then thumped the sleeping Cal on the top of his head. "Wake up and go to bed!" she giggled.

"Huh? What?" Caltus Talienson, former soldier, stirred from his dreams of battle and was pleased to find himself snug beside a warm fire and friends.

"I said . . . Wake-up-and-go-to-bed!"

"Ho! brilliant joke," snorted Cal. He looked at the fire and then put his stone back in a pouch at his belt and sheathed his jewelled sword, a piece of booty from the battle at Cairngorm. "It must be late . . . I suppose Endril's off in the woods again?"

Hathor nodded.

"He's got to be crazy," continued Cal, as the three of them made their way to the stairs. "We've never had it so good . . . fine beds with clean sheets to sleep on, and he spends his nights in the forest."

Bith pinched out her candle and slid willingly under the covers. She had to agree with Cal about these beds. She hadn't slept this well for a long time. Not since the days in her mother's castle, behind the Mistwall. The hard life of the past year, sleeping out in the open, sometimes on rocky ground, sometimes not at all, now seemed like a bad dream. A gust of cool air blew in through a crack in the window. She closed her eyes and drifted off . . . to a wondrous palace.

The great hall was hung with colorful tapestries and lighted by smoking torches. At the far end of the room, she could see a man seated on a golden throne. He motioned her to come forward, and she floated toward him. Somehow this man looked familiar. He had a thin face, a short pointed beard, and was wrapped in white fur robes. A satin cushion appeared and she settled into it. The man smiled pleasantly at her. Suddenly she knew who it was! It was the brother of Odin, king of the Northern gods. The very god who had brought the four outcasts together and sent them into danger.

"Vili!" Bith exclaimed.

The richly dressed man winced at this common greeting, but swallowed his pride with an effort. "You may forego addressing me as Magnificent Lord, Exalted Master, and

Ruler of the Twelve Spheres this time, Elizebith. It has been a long time since we have talked." His voice was all sweetness.

Bith jumped up off the pillow and the dream began to fade. Vili stood up quickly and spoke.

"No, no. Hear me out. Once again I have need of my followers, and there is not time to lose!"

"I'm not going to listen to you any more," snapped Bith. "You promised us great rewards if we would visit that wizard and destroy your stupid sword . . . and what did we get? Nothing! The wizard was a fake and we had to fight Schlein and the Dark Lord's army! You lied to us!"

"Did not Cal receive his father's banner?" soothed the god. "And did you not come into a handsome supply of magical goods? And have you not rested in ease and comfort these last few months?"

"I would hardly call a run down inn in a tiny forest village the lap of luxury," snapped Bith. "I was born a princess and lived in a palace. I was waited upon by servants. And, and . . . a ragged piece of cloth and a few bags of herbs are not what I consider a great reward! Nor was there anything at all for Hathor or Endril!"

"Endril has been very happy of late, in the beech forest, and as for your troll, Hathor is a simple creature and his needs are few . . . . But enough of the past. This time I can do more for you. Since you four managed to destroy the first Runesword, I now have more power. But others remain, and must be retrieved. There will be great things for you all at the end of this adventure."

"No, no, I won't listen to you any more!" screeched Bith. She scrunched up her face and turned away. The great hall disappeared and she landed on the floor with a thump, tangled in her own blankets.

"Oof!" she said, as she sat up painfully and composed

her thoughts. "He will not get to me this time!" she resolved. She stood up and remade her bed, tucking the blankets neatly in at the corners and then sat on it, and stared out through the window into the cold spring night. She thought she could make out the shadowy form of Endril, approaching through the trees. Her head nodded slowly and she fell into a dreamless sleep.

The elf, Endril, leaned against his favorite tree, oblivious to the chill night air, and wrapped his arms about his knees. This was a young and healthy beech forest and it was happy to have him among it. Endril was glad he had helped to keep the Dark Lord's Mistwall from this place, even if the setback the four had caused at Cairngorm was only temporary. His thoughts drifted back to forests of long ago, now lost forever behind the Mistwall. He shut his eyes and breathed deeply.

A great forest . . . a blue haze, perhaps an early morning fog filled the air, and the forest was old and tall . . . . Endril wandered among the mighty oaks which whispered to him peacefully in ancient voices.

"Come forward, Endril," murmured a particularly gnarled old tree, barely visible through the mist, "come and be seated in the soft grass at my feet."

The elf made his way around some bushes and a fallen log and then sat down, contemplating the tree that had spoken. For a moment there was silence, but as he stared at the trunk a face appeared on the bark. He blinked, and it became clearer. Yes, there it was, a pair of eyes, a nose, a mouth . . . even a small beard. It was the face he had seen before reflected in water and later on a sword. A cynical grin appeared on Endril's face as he spoke.

"Well, if it isn't the Exalted Master, Vili, Ruler of the Twelve Spheres!" The elf bowed slightly.

"Good," replied the face in the tree. "I knew I could count on a little respect from you! I trust you have been enjoying your stay in Cairnwald."

"It has been pleasant enough, Magnificent Lord." Endril forced himself to utter the last compliment. Vili had done little for the four besides get them into trouble. And the treasures he had promised for the destruction of the Runesword at Cairngorm had not materialized. Endril shrugged. He knew that it was better to soothe Vili's ego than insult him.

"Fine, now let us talk some business. I find that once again I have need of my servants. There is mischief afoot in the land of—"

"You expect us to go on another errand for you, Master?" interrupted Endril, struggling to be polite.

The tree shook its leaves, as though struck by a sudden breeze.

"Of course," snapped Vili. "Now if you will let me finish what I have to say . . ."

"Yet, as I recall, there were certain promises made to a group of outcasts you called together many months ago. . . ."

"Promises that will be kept!" boomed Vili in a deeper voice, accompanied by an ever greater shaking of leaves.

"I know I am asleep," said the elf quickly. "And now I choose to awaken, for we have resolved not to listen to any more of your promises!" He stood up.

"No! wait!"

Endril awoke with a shiver and held his arms close to his body for warmth. He was standing now, and the cold filled his body. Suddenly the thought of the warmth of the inn seemed very attractive and he began making his way back through the forest. As he came out into a clearing, he could see the building in the distance. On the second floor, through the window, he could just make out a dark form—Bith, staring directly at him as though he were expected.

The troll, Hathor, turned restlessly on his mat of straw. He had been too large for any bed in the inn, but was quite content to sleep on the floor. It mattered little to him. But tonight he was having trouble sleeping. Distant images from the past kept flashing through his mind images of bones and blood, of death and dying, and the dank, dark troll caves he had abandoned long ago.

All at once the images crystallized into the form of a large, pale troll. A troll with red hair like his own, standing in a well-lit cave. The troll spoke to Hathor in a strange voice. A voice he had heard before in his sleep.

"Welcome, Hathor. There is a great task to be performed, and I am in need of the services of a good and kindly troll such as yourself."

Hathor scratched his hair with his fingers and squinted sideways at his dream. The narrow nose, those eyes, and the little red beard.

"Now I know!" exclaimed the troll. "You, Vili! Go away! Bith say not to speak to you!"

Hathor let out a loud yelp and sat up abruptly in the dark. His elbow knocked a small table across the room with a clatter. Cal was sitting up in his bed, looking at him.

"What is it, Hathor?" asked the boy.

"The voice . . . Vili—" He fumbled for words. "—he want us to do something."

"I know," replied Cal as he stood. "I was just visited by him myself. Let's see if he's gotten to Bith." The two of them stepped out into the dimly lit hallway and hurried toward Bith's room. Cal stopped suddenly and Hathor bumped into him from behind.

"Ouch!"

Elizebith of Morea was standing there in the darkened corridor before them. Endril appeared out of the darkness and joined them. The four stared at each other for a moment and then Bith brushed past Endril and started down the stairs.

"Let's go down and throw some logs on the fire and talk about this." She spoke with authority. As the foursome clumped down the stairs, the landlord pulled open his door and watched them descend. He muttered something under his breath, yawned, and then slammed the door shut behind him.

CHAPTER
2

The fire flickered brightly with renewed vigor, eagerly consuming the wood Hathor had thrown upon it. The four companions huddled close to the welcome blaze, to drive away the cold, and possibly put a little more distance between themselves and Vili, since the god was only able to manifest himself to them in cold objects . . . a pool of water, the blade of a sword. Now, much to their displeasure, he had worked his way into their dreams. Each, in turn, described their encounter with the god.

"I had hoped we were done with him," said Bith flatly. "I mean, he hasn't spoken to any of us in months."

"It was just a matter of time," answered Endril in a solemn voice. "I knew he would come after us again. I don't think he'll give up until we've destroyed all of his Runeswords."

Elizebith stood up with her back to the fire and addressed the others with her hands on her hips. "We're not going to work for him again! We've already agreed!"

"Then why are the four of us still together?" asked the elf.

"Because . . . because we have come to be friends!" The others nodded agreement. Bith began to pace back and forth, her hands locked behind her. "But it's going to be difficult to sleep, to live . . . if Vili keeps popping into our dreams!"

"Maybe we go south, to warmer place," suggested Hathor.

Cal rose and followed in Bith's footsteps, circling the room. "We've been here way too long anyway," he said. "I haven't crossed swords with anyone for so long I may have forgotten how. And when's the last time you cast a spell, Bith? It's time we were back on the road."

"Somewhere warm," the girl mumbled, half to herself.

Endril shook his head in disgust. "Do you seriously think we can run away from a god? Vili will follow us wherever we go and whatever we do."

"We can try," snapped Bith. "I, for one, do not want to tangle with the forces of the Dark Lord again. Heroic deeds deserve rich rewards. Vili was very stingy when it came time to reward us." She stopped pacing and put her hands on her hips. "I say we leave this very morning!"

"And how will we live?" asked Endril curtly. "I'm sure the innkeeper does not intend to follow us with a wagon and cook for us each day!"

"We will live by our wits, as we did before! Besides, we have a few coins . . . and we're a damned good team. We're capable of taking care of ourselves!"

Hathor was on his feet, fumbling at his waist. He produced a pouch and pulled out a shiny object. It was the silver crescent that had belonged to the wizard of Cairngorm, which he had found at the bottom of the crag. He stuffed it in Elizebith's hand. "We have silver too! It time! We go south!"

"Well, I must confess that I think we've lingered here too long and that we should indeed move on . . . . But do you have any particular goal in mind?'' queried Endril, still seated with his legs crossed.

''Well, no, but we'll think of something,'' answered Bith. ''The important thing is to get going, and soon!''

''Ahem!'' said a voice from the top of the stairs. It was the landlord, leaning over the rail, his eyes fairly glowing in the firelight. ''I could not help but overhear your problem. If you will be so kind as to allow me to make a suggestion, I think I can help you.'' He began to shuffle down the stairs. ''There's a fine hot spring, a place called Baoancaster, not much more than a fortnight's journey from here. They've warm mineral water baths all year round!'' He paused and as nobody replied, he continued, ''Now let me go into the kitchen and fetch you all some breakfast! I can tell you more about the place.''

The first rays of the early morning sun were touching the outstretched barren fingers of the treetops when Endril returned from bidding a fond farewell to the beechwood forest, and joined the small crowd on the dusty road gathered before the inn. The four outcasts, with their bundles on their backs, were ready to leave. The innkeeper and his wife and a group of barefooted children were gathered around to bid them farewell.

The sky was blue and clear and in the west, opposite the sun, the few puffy clouds were still bathed in a golden light. Cal shivered in the cool morning air, pulling his cloak tight around his neck for warmth. Beneath those clouds, he thought, and not far beyond the forest, lurked the evil Mistwall. At the very least, they would be moving farther away from the horrid thing.

The landlord and his wife had packed a bag filled with dried meat, fruit, and bread, and Hathor tossed this easily over his huge shoulders, thanking his hosts with a wide, toothy grin. Bith hugged the innkeeper's wife one last time and then they were under way, with Endril quickly taking the lead. Soon the small village was left behind them. For some time they traveled silently down the road, which wound gently among the leafless trees of the forest with Endril far ahead, Cal following as fast as he could, then Bith, and Hathor bringing up the rear. They stopped briefly while Cal stepped into the woods to cut a long, straight branch. Deftly, he stripped the twigs from the sides and fashioned himself a walking stick. When the foursome resumed their trek, the silence was accompanied by a steady thump, thump as his stick beat upon the dirt track.

The sun was fully up now, and its warmth was especially welcome to Bith, who had been walking swiftly, clutching a black shawl close around her shoulders to keep out the cold. They breasted a small hill and stepped aside for a young boy who guided a bumping, jerking oxcart along the road toward the village. He smiled and waved as he recognized the four heroes of Cairngorm and two small heads popped out of the pile of straw in the back of the cart and cheered them.

Cal broke the silence. "Well, that may be the last of that! Where we're going we'll not be the big heroes anymore."

"Little fish in a big pond," remarked Bith almost sadly as they started down the slope. She was going to miss her warm bed with real sheets. But then they would be of no use to her if she couldn't sleep because Vili filled her dreams.

At the bottom of the valley, they crossed a clear stream, and Hathor took a few moments searching under the damp forest litter, producing a paw full of white, carrot-like roots. The track climbed steeply again and as the four trudged along slowly, the thump of Cal's stick was now punctuated with sharp crunches as Hathor munched on his snacks.

By noon they had left the hardwood forest behind them and were descending into a deep glacial valley lined on each side with tall green pine trees that whispered quietly in the wind. A silver ribbon of a stream wound back and forth across the flat bottom of the valley and the land on either side was covered with hedgerows and dotted with neat little farm houses. Endril paused at a crossroad and examined a signpost, which leaned drunkenly to one side. One of the two signs it wore pointed west and read "Cairngorm."

"Not much left of that place," he commented, dryly.

"Or castle," added Hathor. During the course of their great adventure last fall, the castle of Cairngorm had tumbled off a ledge into the rift below and they had narrowly escaped with their lives.

"But there are good people there, so let us hope they have rebuilt what was left of their village," said Cal. There was silence again as they relived the bloody struggle with orcs, men, slugs, and the treacherous giant, Backbreaker.

Then Bith broke the spell and touched the sign pointing east. "Here lies our path, Baoancaster. Let's be on our way . . . I can feel the warm waters of the baths now."

"I can feel the weight of this pack on my back," complained Cal, adjusting the load he carried.

"Hah! You get soft over winter," laughed Hathor, nudging Cal with his big fist and grinning wickedly.

They set out again, along the road that clung to the side of the valley, working their way slowly downhill, occasionally passing the small cottage of a peasant, or woodsman. The evergreens now alternated with leafless hardwood trees, and the bright sun almost made the early spring day warm. It seemed the farther away they got from the Mistwall, the happier the country became.

At length, hunger overcame the group. Endril led them off the track to a pleasant meadow filled with early-blooming wildflowers. A tiny brook gurgled behind them as they partook of the contents of the food bag.

Dusk came, and they stopped at a clearing beside the road and Hathor built a warm fire. Bith and Cal complained about their sore limbs, much to the troll's amusement, and Endril shook his head in disgust and disappeared into the darkness, as was his custom. The night was clear, cool, star-filled, and quiet.

Morning brought the glad news that none had been visited in dream by Vili.

"Maybe he lose us!" said Thor, dropping a dry log on the coals from the night before.

"I certainly hope so," added Cal as he rolled his blanket and stuffed it into his pack. "If we're to have another adventure, we can have it without him!"

Bith stretched and rubbed a sore leg muscle. "I knew going south would do the trick. The farther we get from Vili, the happier I'll be."

"And I think you are all crazy," said Endril as he emerged from the woods. "Vili will find us no matter where we go. Mark my words . . . there's a Runesword in our future."

"Don't you ever have anything positive to say?" snapped Bith. "Vili did not come to us last night, and I have a feeling that he will not be in our dreams again at all!"

"Well, I hope your feeling proves right." Endril's tone implied otherwise. "Now, Hathor, where's the food? Let's eat!"

The weather stayed clear and fair over the next several days and the foursome grew more cheerful as they wound their way down out of the highlands and along the stony foothills toward the plains. No more was heard from Vili. They began to practice some of their old battle orders and

formations, stopping now and then to fight imaginary ene-
mies in mock combat . . . The three fighters in a circle with
Bith in the middle ready to cast spells.

To sharpen her skills, Elizebith of Morea practiced casting
a few spells. First she set fire to an old stump and Hathor
had to stomp out the flames which threatened to spread to
a nearby field. Later, she enlarged a fieldmouse, which then
proceeded to chase them around a cornfield till Hathor turned
and lopped its head off with his axe. Finally she levitated
the entire group up a small cliff. It took everyone but Endril
half a day to climb back down.

The food the innkeeper gave them soon ran out, and they
stopped at a farm, trading some wood chopping and stump
removal for bread and a small pig. Hathor agreed to roast
the animal for the others, but he himself stuck to his pre-
dominately vegetarian ways and would eat none of it, pre-
ferring to crunch on the roots he found, of which there
seemed to be an unending supply.

At the end of a fortnight they found themselves huddled
together beneath a large oak tree, hiding from a rainstorm.
It was a thick forest not two days travel from Baoancaster.
After the rain stopped, a thin, reedy voice spoke to them,
seemingly out of nowhere.

"Caloo, calee, you there beneath yon tree;
Mina, sina, kuusikoll, I see one of you is a troll!"

Cal drew his sword and Endril slipped silently into the
woods. "Who are you? Where are you?" demanded Bith,
turning in all directions. Hathor readied his axe and stood
by her side. There was no answer. Moments later Endril
returned.

"It must be some kind of magic," he whispered. "I found
nothing!"

"You think it was Vili?" asked Cal.

"No, Vili needs a vessel in which to manifest himself to us . . . and the silly rhyme."

"Maybe he used raindrops," suggested the boy.

"Ooh, I hope not!" said Bith, as she looked warily this way and that. And then the voice spoke again.

"Naelta, mailta, sina jaat siihen;
I'll be back soon, I'll see you then."

There was a rustle in the bushes that sounded like footsteps. Once again Endril darted away in hot pursuit.

"Bith, haven't you got some kind of spell to make this thing show itself?" asked Cal.

"I don't know what it is, or where to cast a spell, even if I had a spell for this situation." She frowned. "Which I don't."

Once again Endril returned, frustrated and empty handed. "Enough of this foolishness. The rain has stopped, let's be on our way and leave the voice behind." The rest quickly agreed and they picked their way back to the track, which was now a sea of mud, and resumed their journey. For a time they struggled along in the ruts, then Endril led them back into the woods, where the going was easier. They heard no more from the mysterious voice.

Just as the sun came out again, the elf stopped suddenly and pointed off to the left.

"Look, there, did you see it?"

"See what?" asked Cal.

"There was something moving beyond the trees . . . and I saw a glint of red. We're not alone!"

"You're seeing things!" exclaimed Bith, anxious to be on her way, and equally anxious for it not to be true. "The woods are full of birds, you saw the breast of a robin!"

She shoved Cal, who was in front of her, and continued on along through the litter of dead leaves that carpeted the ground.

"That was no robin," contended Endril. He searched the area carefully, looking for any signs, but could find nothing. "You take the lead, Cal, and stay near the road. I'll return soon." The elf disappeared into some underbrush, determined to search out that which he had seen.

"Well there's a fine how-do-you-do!" exclaimed Bith, pulling her hair back from her eyes and tossing it over her shoulder. Cal was just standing there, staring after the elf. Hathor waited a moment and then crunched through the forest litter, circled around the boy and was soon followed by Bith.

Finding himself alone, Cal came to his senses. "Hey, wait for me!" he cried, and trotted off after his companions. They traveled for some time, with Hathor in the lead, until they came to a broad stream which was too deep for them to cross. Unable to find a shallow ford they struck back toward the road, and were surprised to find Endril, sitting on a stone bridge, waiting for them.

"There's something out there . . . and it is following us," he said matter-of-factly.

"Nonsense!" snapped Bith, but she looked over her shoulder, nonetheless.

The foursome moved on, with Endril pacing more slowly than ever, looking cautiously from side to side. Apparently Hathor had also seen the thing, for Bith noticed that the troll had unslung his axe again and was holding it in front of him, at the ready.

Suddenly, a small figure rushed out of the bushes and stood in the road before them. It had the face of a man, but was wrinkled as though with great age, and its skin looked leathery and tough. The little creature sported a long fluffy grey beard, and slung across his shoulders, a grey cloak. A gay, red, pointed cap was perched on the top of his head. Tall, shiny black boots, grey pants, and a homespun shirt completed his outfit. The newcomer bowed, his face wreathed in a wide smile.

"Do not be alarmed, gentle folk. Allow me to introduce myself. I am Gunnar Greybeard of Glasvellir Hall. In short, a dwarf from Northunderland."

"Never heard of the place," said Endril.

"And what do you want with us?" Bith asked, with obvious hostility.

"Ho, sweet lady, calm your fires," soothed the dwarf. "Here, please accept this little gift as a token of my good will." He pulled a gold coin out of his belt and handed it to Bith.

She eyed both sides of the coin with suspicion. "Why would you give us a gold coin?"

"Pshoo, do you not know 'tis good luck to accept a gift from a dwarf?" The little fellow winked at her and continued, "And if that is not reason enough, you may consider it a reward for services rendered!"

"A reward? For what?" Bith handed the coin to Hathor who bit it and nodded, smiling.

"Why, for my rescue, of course," answered Gunnar with a grin. "If the four of you hadn't come along and stood under that tree, I might still be trapped in its branches." He waved a hand in a broad northward sweep. "Where I come from, there are troll witches of great power, and I fear I ran afoul of the worst of them. Loviatar is her name."

Hathor's eyes lit up with interest.

"She put me under a charm, turned me into a pebble, and threw me across the ocean. I landed in that tree. And I would as like have stayed a pebble forever, unless four companions of good heart came together to break the spell

. . . and mind you, one of those companions had to be a troll, or there I would have stayed.'' He produced three more coins and handed them out to the others.

"Here, I have reconsidered. One for each of you. But we tarry too long. Now that I have legs again, I yearn to travel. Perhaps you'll be so kind as to let me join your company on this fine path.''

Bith was reluctant. "Well, I don't know . . . . We've had a bad experience letting a stranger join our group.''

"Only as far as Baoancaster?" suggested Cal.

"Fine!" said the dwarf. "Now tell me your names, so that I may know you all!'' and he set out down the road. Endril smiled and joined him and Cal shrugged his shoulders and followed. Bith sighed noisily and grudgingly walked along in the mud beside Hathor, who was chuckling trollishly to himself.

As they traveled, the dwarf talked incessantly, spinning stories and tales of his beloved homeland. It soon became obvious that he was anxious to return to his ancestral land, and equally anxious that the foursome should come with him.

Later, seated around the campfire, having finished their meal, Gunnar produced a bottle of wine, and the mood grew more relaxed as even Bith began to enjoy herself. Hathor alternately crunched on a root and drank wine. After telling a fable about the cunning fox, the dwarf related some of his own past history, and spoke of a mighty sword named Sjonbrand, the Skryling's blade, that he and the other dwarves of Glasvellir had forged.

Gunnar's eyes lit up with fires from within. "Never had we made such a sword before. Together we brought our best steel and all our talents. Five thousand times we placed it in the fire, and five thousand times we quenched it. Five months we labored. We drew it out and hammered it down five thousand times . . . each time folding in all the magic we knew.''

Cal was entranced and sat with his elbows on his knees, resting his chin on his hands, listening to the dwarf's tale.

The dwarf went on, ''We had tried many times before to forge such a blade and failed, and when, this time, we succeeded we were beside ourselves with joy and pride. Its balance was perfect and the edge could not be dulled. It floated through the air like a feather but dealt blows that would do Thor's hammer proud.''

Bith suddenly frowned and broke in, ''Wait a minute, this sword, this Seeon, er . . .''

''Sjonbrand!''

''Yes, Sjonbrand,'' she continued, ''was it covered with runes?'' Hathor grunted as he realized what she was thinking.

''Of course, my lady,'' came the answer.

''I knew it!'' Bith stood up and stamped angrily. ''And you work for Vili, don't you?''

The dwarf looked dumbfounded and shook his head. ''What do you mean? We dwarves of Glasvellir are a proud and sturdy lot, and we work for no one but our king, Gyrthrym Goldbeard. And who is this Vili you mention?''

''Do you take us for fools? How can you sit there and tell me you have fashioned a Runesword and did not do it for Vili, brother of Odin?''

''Calm yourself, Elizebith,'' said the dwarf, taken aback. ''Every sword forged at Glasvellir Hall is covered with runes. It is our custom. And now that you mention it, I do remember old Gevrym teaching me in my youth of Odin, Vili, and Ve . . . but that was long ago, and I was sent here against my will by the witch, Loviatar.''

Cal drew his sword, taken from the battlefield at Cairngorm, and held it in the firelight. ''Look, Bith, there are runes scribed along even my blade, but it is not a 'Rune-sword' of the type Vili wants.''

"Not every sword is a magic Runesword, filled with the power of Vili!'' added Endril.

It took a while to calm the girl, but their reassuring words and the wine which was passed again and again eventually drew Bith into a mellow, if wary, mood. More tales were told around the glowing fire, and even Endril stayed to listen as the dwarf wove his stories on into the night. Bith, how-ever, curled up in her blanket and fell asleep, still secretly convinced, despite their reassuring words, that the dwarf was a messenger from Vili.

CHAPTER
3

The cowering servants scuttled around the small room, endeavoring, sometimes unsuccessfully, to stay out of the way of the huge man, who thumped around the room in an angry circle. His features, which some might have thought quite pleasant in repose, were now contorted in an angry, black scowl. He stood more than seven feet tall and his immense barrel chest was bare, clothed only with the hundreds of gold ornaments that hung round his thick neck, jingling and clinking as he paced. Every now and then he would mutter something beneath his breath and then slam the fist of one mighty hand into the palm of the other with a resounding thwack. He turned abruptly and smashed his great belly into a clever old woman who had been following in his footsteps to avoid his glare.

"Hellfire and damnation!" he bellowed as he swatted her aside with a huge paw. "Out of my way, slime!" He stomped over to the fireplace, grabbed a six-inch log, snapped it over his knee, and threw it into the flames.

Outside the door, in the hallway, two men waited, unwilling to enter. One was dressed in a blue velvet coat and pants, a plumed, bejewelled hat, and cradled a small ebony box in his arms. The other wore a long red robe, his face was covered with bushy black whiskers, and he held a crystal globe in his hand.

"He's in a fine mood today!" said the one in the blue coat and plumed hat.

"Such a fine mood, Vieno, that I think you should consult with him first!" said the other, indicating the door.

"Oh, no, I wouldn't think of it, the Scryer takes precedence over the Keeper of the Seal!"

The frightened servant who tended the door was obviously hoping that neither of them would decide to enter.

"He's been to see the Dark Lord again, you know," Ormoc the scryer said jokingly.

"Oh, my! I just remembered that I've forgotten something. Do excuse me!" cried the man in the blue coat as he rushed off down the stone passageway, his hat nearly tumbling from his head.

"Your courage, perchance!" taunted Ormoc as his recent companion disappeared around a corner of the corridor. Ormoc turned slowly and addressed the servant. "Well, it's now or never, Griswold. You'd better announce me. I have important news. Let us hope it improves our master's temper."

With terror in his eyes, Griswold clawed the door open and peeped inside. Then with a sudden rush of courage, he disappeared into the chambers of Schlein, evil wizard, Exalted Master, supreme among men, and second in power only to the Dark Lord himself.

Ormoc backed away from the door, knowing what would come next. A moment later, the door burst open with a bang and Griswold flew out into the hall, head first, to land with a thud on the floor at the scryer's feet. The servant looked up, half dazed, and bleated, "He'll see you now, you may go in!"

The scryer swallowed hard and then strode into the stuffy room with a deliberate, stilted gait, trying to look as professional as possible.

"What do you bring me, Ormoc, more bad news?" Schlein banged his great fist down on a wooden table and glared at his underling. Ormoc stopped in front of the huge man and craned his neck to look into his master's eyes.

"On the contrary, Exalted Master, the watching is over, and that which you have sought for so long can now be attained." Ormoc pulled a small cushion out from within his robe and plopped it on the table, carefully placing the crystal globe upon it.

"What news? What news?" demanded the bulky giant. "Chairs! Bring us chairs, that we may sit!" Servants rushed hither and thither, producing a carved wooden throne for their master and a small stool for Ormoc.

"She has left the enchanted wood. She is now beyond the protection of the charm." Ormoc began waving his hands rythmically over the crystal and a blue haze began to appear over the table that stood between the two men. In the haze a human form materialized, that of a beautiful young woman with striking silver eyes, walking in the sunlight, a black shawl clutched around her shoulders. Her face was pale and finely formed and her long dark hair glistened in the light as it cascaded over her shoulders.

"Morea!" boomed Schlein, angrily. "Why do you show me that witch!" He stood up, knocking his carved throne over onto the stone floor. "I'll have you . . ."

"It's *Elizebith*! Not Morea!" screamed Ormoc as he ducked to avoid the blow that was sure to follow. The image faded from the mist, and then the mist was gone.

Schlein froze, fist clenched in mid-air, and his eyes went

wide as the full import of the scryer's words struck home.
Elizebith, seventeen-year-old daughter of Morea, yet all but
indistinguishable from her mother. An evil smile crept
across his face. Elizebith, spoiler of all his plans. Elizebith,
the one most responsible for his ignominious defeat at Cairngorm. Elizebith, the one who had brought the wrath of the
Dark Lord down upon him.

Elizebith, who would be his bride . . . .

Suddenly the enormous man grabbed Ormoc by the shoulders, lifted him off his feet and shook him like a rag doll.
"You have done well, Ormoc. You have gained favor with
me." Schlein dropped the trembling scryer to the floor and
continued speaking. "I want you to watch and follow her.
Report to me of her movements. But do *not,* I repeat do
not lose her! I do not have to remind you of the consequences
should such a thing happen. Now begone, I have evil to
work!"

Ormoc gathered his crystal and retreated as quickly as he
could with dignity, asking himself for the millionth time if
he was in the right line of work. On the way out, he stumbled
over Griswold, who still lay moaning in a heap on the floor.

Later that day, Schlein sent a vile flying creature to summon the black dragon, and called a group of sinister char-
acters, few of which were human, into conference. Many
unpleasant plans were made.

CHAPTER
4

Endril awakened to the rich smell of cooked food. It was most unusual for him to have fallen asleep in camp. The dwarf sat tending a brace of rabbits as they roasted on sticks over the fire, and on the ground beside him was what appeared to be a pile of carrots and potatoes. How curious that the dwarf had accomplished all this without waking him.

Gunnar noticed Endril stirring. "Top of the morning to you, master Endril, I hope I did not disturb you, as you can see I have gathered a little of nature's bounty. One must not be a burden to one's hosts!"

Hathor and Cal sat up and took in the unexpected but welcome sight.

"Very strange," said Bith, rubbing her eyes. "Where did all that food come from?"

"Strange indeed," commented Endril, "for I sleep but lightly and there is little that slips past me in the night; yet look at all this."

"Most likely he conjured it up just now!" declared the

girl, with a frown of suspicion. "More of Vili's trick-ery. . . ."

Gunnar's face twisted in a mock grimace, and he pulled at his grey whiskers. "Now, now, fair lady, nothing's amiss. That was heady wine I poured for you last night. Perhaps it was a bit too strong." He pointed into the sky, the sun was high overhead. "See, the hour is late."

Endril jumped to his feet in disbelief, squinting at the sky, "Strong wine, or strong magic, or both . . . we've lost half a day!"

"Strong wine," reiterated the dwarf. "Kultani-kalihini! I had plenty of time to trap these creatures and dig up some roots at the farm down the way." He produced a fresh loaf of bread from a sack at his side. "And the good farmer's wife gave me this when I blessed her milk cow! You should know 'tis good luck to accept a gift from a dwarf!"

Hathor reached over and grabbed a handful of potatoes, popped one in his mouth and began to crunch. "Mmm, taste good, indeed. Thank you, Gunnar Greybeard."

The dwarf gestured at the repast. "Help yourselves, my newfound friends!"

Cal wasted no time grabbing a roasted rabbit for himself. Hathor went to work on the carrots, while Endril broke the crusty loaf apart. Bith sulked and complained, but was soon overwhelmed by hunger. The enthusiasm with which her companions ate was contagious. Too much so, she thought to herself as she picked delicately and distainfully at the meat, as though she was doing the dwarf a favor, unwilling to reveal her very real hunger.

Not long after they had finished their meal and resumed their journey they came to the top of a low, treeless hill. The group paused and took in the view. There before them, in the afternoon sun, spread a broad, peaceful valley, cov-ered with a yellow-and-brown patchwork of farms and an occasional copse of evergreens. There were roads and villages to be seen as well, and on the far side, through the blue haze of distance, they could make out a tower or castle that sat atop a strange, wooded mound.

"I wonder if that's Baoancaster?" mused Bith.

"We'll find out soon enough." Endril was still staring at the strange castle.

"Maybe they'll know," said Cal, pointing down the road. A small group of travelers was laboring up the hill. There were four men, and as they drew near, it could be seen that the leader was a large man clad in a long, drab, green robe. He was bald and leaned on a staff topped with odd carvings as he puffed along the trail. The other three were raggedly clothed and heavily burdened by large bundles which they bore on their backs.

The big man stopped to catch his breath and then addressed the group. "Greetings, fellow travelers! A beautiful day to be abroad, yes?" His three weary companions sank gratefully to the side of the road with a common moan and leaned against their packs.

"Aye, that it is, good sir," answered the dwarf.

The big man stumped his strange staff in the ground. "I am Brother Clement, and I travel to the mountains to meditate and communicate with the gods. And where might yourselves to bound?"

"We seek the baths of Baoancaster!"

"Ah, a fine place indeed." Clement rubbed the top of his bald head with his free hand. "A sure cure for the little ills that trouble our mortal bodies. I've been there many a time myself, but these days it is a cure for spiritual ill that I seek . . ." His voice trailed off and his eyes widened as he noticed Hathor, realizing that he was not a human, but a troll. In spite of the hat and human clothing, Hathor was hard to miss, but it had been a while since his appearance

had made such an impression on someone. This seemed to
please rather than dismay the troll.

Bith noticed Clement's reaction and stepped in front of
her friend. "We were wondering," she said, smoothly dis-
tracting the man, "if that castle on the horizon marked our
goal?"

"What . . . oh!" stuttered the big man. He turned and
shuddered visibly. "Goodness, no! You want to stay away
from that place. That's the tower of Murcroft, himself.
Certes you've heard of him!"

"No," answered Bith. "Who or what is Murcroft?"

"A sort of a wizard, and a ne'er-do-well for sure. There's
those who say he favors the Dark Lord, and would summon
the Mistwall upon this fine valley. The woods around his
tower are rife with thieves and brigands who prey on the
travelers on the Great West Road. . . . See it there."

Bith could see nothing. Endril nodded silently.

"Oh, yes," remarked the dwarf.

Clement swept his hand in the other direction, farther
west, "Off there, in yon hills lies Baoancaster, a good safe
distance from Murcroft and his doings. There, see the smoke
and steam rising on the horizon? You're a good two days
from it yet."

Clement inquired as to the safety of the road ahead and
they talked a while longer. Bith casually mentioned Cairngorm and the holy man bubbled with excitement, greatly
impressed to discover he was in the presence of the four
heroes, who were spoken of so often in the news from the
north.

At last Clement decided it was time to part company.
The big man had to kick his three servants to wake them
from sleep. The raggedy men groaned and complained as
they lifted their unwieldy burdens, and then the holy man

and his "mules" marched off, leaving the heroes alone with the dwarf atop the hill.

"Shall we?" smiled the dwarf as he gestured forward, and the four, plus one, again took to the road. Gunnar Greybeard broke into a long fable about a king of the north and his ship that sailed in the skies. Bith frowned and tried not to listen, but soon in spite of her efforts, found herself caught up in the story.

The tale went on and the miles went by. They were unaware of passing travelers and stopped no more for drink or rest. The companions marched through one village and then another, and saw not the faces that stared at them from windows and doors. A beggar asked for money and then cursed the group as they walked past, unheeding.

A great knight and his squire rode by and Cal took no notice, so compelling was the spell of the tale. It was a timeless trek of which only Endril seemed even dimly aware. And then, as the sun turned into a great orange ball resting on the edge of the horizon, Gunnar's story abruptly ended. And, waking as though from a dream, they found themselves in the middle of the town of Baoancaster, standing in front of the Inn of the Roasted Swan.

Bith was up to her neck in a pool of steaming water, clad only in her undershift with Endril lazing at her side. She was watching Hathor, Cal, and the dwarf, who sat in another pool across the stone-floored room, deeply involved in yet another of Gunnar's tales. He was rambling on about a singing sword. She turned away in disgust. Swords, swords, swords. That's all they ever talked about.

"I don't like this the least little bit," she complained. "There's something fishy about that dwarf and the tricks he plays with our minds. Look at the way he goes on . . . we've practically lost Cal and Hathor to the creature."

"He's magic," said the elf, turning slowly in the water beside her, "of that there is no denying. And I still wonder . . ."

"It's Vili! I know it! He sent this stupid dwarf to torment us because we wouldn't let him into our dreams."

"So now you agree with me. I told you he would not leave us alone. Yet, I'm not sure this dwarf is from Vili. And as for his tormenting us, even you must admit that his magic has only helped us on our journey." The elf looked her in the eyes and smiled impishly. "Who was it who insisted that we head south anyway!"

"Ooh, you're as impossible as the others!" She whipped her hand and splashed Endril in the face. Bith climbed angrily out of the water, wrapped herself in a towel and stormed off, bare feet slapping on the wet stones. Endril laughed and then rolled over, leaning his elbows on the side of the pool so he could listen as Greybeard's story unfolded.

Ormoc sat alone in the darkened chamber, breathing heavily as he watched the image in the mist before him. Maybe his job was not so bad after all. Two weeks of peering unseen at the lovely Elizebith of Morea had been quite pleasant indeed. He squirmed in his chair as Bith dropped her towel to the floor, and removed her clinging shift, revealing herself in all her glory. Oh yes, being a scryer had its moments. He groaned as the girl stretched her naked body across the bed. He could never have Elizebith for himself. That he knew with certainty, but he could have moments with her that no one else could share. Moments only he would know.

If Schlein had any idea what his scryer was up to . . . Ormoc shook his head, trying to banish that unpleasant thought. There was a knock on the door, and Ormoc jumped to his feet, with his heart in his throat. How could Schlein know? The image of Bith and the mist faded abruptly. Ormoc plumped his black beard and shook his head.

"Get a hold of yourself, man!" he said quietly, and then walked over to the door in the dim candlelight. "Yes, what is it?" he answered, with as much composure as he could muster.

"Murcroft wants ta see ya!" came a small voice from the other side of the door.

"I'll be right up!" Ormoc carefully packed his crystal in a cushioned box and then hurried up the winding stair behind the orc. He was nearly breathless when he reached the wizard, who was seated with a group of burly men.

"Ah, Ormoc! Is she still there?"

"Yes, at the Inn of the Roasted Swan, along with her four companions."

"Good! They'll be no problem."

For some reason, the barkeep was being difficult that night, and refused to let Hathor into his hall. Bith's protestations, and Cal's threats had no effect other than to summon three heavy-set, frowning men who stood before them with their legs spread and their arms crossed. Gunnar Greybeard, who arrived late, worked his way through the throng at the door.

"Hey Ho, Pala tuli-o . . . what seems to be the problem here?"

"No trolls allowed!" growled the barkeep in an angry voice.

"What's gone awrong can be made awright!" The dwarf slipped something into the barman's hand, and the man's frown brightened into a smile. He turned away from the door and motioned for his three friends to follow. Gunnar addressed Cal and Hathor. "There now, what's your pleasure? Let's take a seat and drink our measure!"

The three of them wound through the crowd of merry-makers to a table in a dark corner, without even looking to see if Endril and Bith were following.

Bith was beside herself. "Would you look at that! What happened to the four of us . . . the four heroes of Cairngorm? The four friends?"

"Don't worry, all things pass," soothed Endril. He took the girl by the arm and led her to a table by the fire. A minstrel was seated nearby singing a sad love ballad, and the crowd was just quiet enough for them to hear the words. It was a song of a maiden whose lover had gone to sea and never returned, but she waited and waited faithfully. A tear came to Bith's eye, and she wondered if she would ever have a love like the one in the song.

Her glance rested on Endril, seated there in front of her. His features were pleasant, even handsome, but Endril was more like a brother than a prospective lover. For that matter, so was Cal . . . and even Hathor.

She looked over at the table in the dark corner where the two hung on every word that issued from Gunnar's mouth! Her mellow thoughts faded away and in an instant she was angry again. Fortunately a mug of ale landed on the table in front of her and she gulped it down without a thought as to where it came from or who had paid for it.

The evening wore on, and the drinks kept flowing. The crowd drowned out the minstrel, who gave up and started drinking, along with everyone else. Occasionally Bith glanced over at the three who sat in the corner table, but her face felt numb and she was no longer angry. She even laughed when Hathor fell off his stool and had to be helped up by Cal and the dwarf.

Endril alone drank only moderately and seemed uneasy, and was not very good conversation as he lapsed into mono-syllables. Somehow the talk, what there was of it, turned

to the wand Bith had found in the ravine below castle Cairngorm. She reached down into a pouch that hung from her
yellow belt and pulled it forth.

"I've really been afraid to use it," she said with a hiccup.
"I've stared at this thing all winter long, trying to figure it
out." She hiccupped again and stared crosseyed at Endril.
"In fact, I don't really think it is a wand!"

She dropped it on the table with a clank that brought
interested stares from those seated nearby. Endril deftly
scooped up the silvery device and hid it in his belt. A
commotion broke out at the door, and there was much yell-
ing and shouting. Endril turned in time to face a group of
armored men, who were pushing their way through the
throng, heading straight for him.

"There she is! Seize her at once!"

Endril went for his knife but a drunk fleeing the soldiers
crashed into him, knocking him aside, and then the men
were all over Bith, who was only half aware of what was
going on. The elf cried out to her, but it was too late. The
place was tightly packed, there was no way to escape. Endril
tried to pull Bith free only to find himself held firmly in the
grasp of several strong men.

"Don't interfere in business what's not yer own," cautioned a harsh voice.

Two haughty-looking officials dressed in officious garb,
marched into the middle of the crowded barroom. One unrolled a scroll while the other beat on a drum to command
silence. The drumroll stopped and the man with the scroll
mounted a chair and began to speak in a high voice.

"O yeas! O yeas! O yeas! It has come to the attention
of the lord mayor of Baoancaster that the vile witch, responsible for the recent plague, the cursing of our chickens,
and the nagging of our wives, is even now among us in the

person of this woman!'' A pause. "Now summon the witchpricker!''

A murmur rushed through the crowd, then a bent old man
with long grey hair limped across the floor. He looked
around and smiled, revealing his last remaining tooth, and
then held up a rather nasty device that looked to Endril
much like a dagger. The elf struggled again, but four strong
hands still gripped him tightly.

"Be good now, master elf!'' came the voice in his ear,
"an' we might just let you go free.''

The speaker with the scroll droned on, ". . . and if this
device shall pierce the breast of this woman causing no
wound, she shall be proved a witch!''

Endril wondered what it would do to her, or any woman,
if she wasn't a witch. The mood of the crowd grew ugly.
An evil cheer was raised. Bith, realizing her danger at last,
struggled and kicked to no avail. The soldiers wrestled her
down onto a table and held her. The old man stepped up
to her, and with a flourish plunged the nasty device into her
breast. Bith screamed, Endril shuddered, and the crowd fell
silent. Then slowly, the man pulled the blade out of Bith's
body. There was no blood on the silver surface.

The old man touched her breast carefully, and jumped
up and down, cackling, "No wound! No wound! She lives!
She's a witch!'' The throng in the bar burst into a frenzy
of madness. "Burn the witch!'' "Kill the witch!'' "Drown
the witch!'' "Ride her out of town on a rail!'' Endril
watched helplessly as Elizebith was dragged, screaming,
from the room. Finally the soldiers released him. Most of
the customers followed the angry mob, leaving the elf all
but alone.

He hurried over to the table in the dark corner and surveyed the carnage with dismay. Cal lay passed out on the
floor, and Hathor was slumped across the table with his

face buried in a plate of food. Gunnar looked up at Endril with bleary eyes, totally unaware of what had taken place only moments ago.

"Theesh guysh have no capashity for strong dring!" said the dwarf as he slid under the table and landed on the floor beside Cal.

CHAPTER
5

Endril left his unconscious companions in the tavern and slipped quietly out into the night. It was not difficult to pick up the trail of those who had carried off Bith, and the elf followed discreetly in the shadows. If he could not rescue her, at least he would see what they planned to do with her.

The angry mob, some of its number carrying torches, wound up and around the twisted, hilly streets of Baoancaster and eventually stopped before a large stone building. The soldiers had taken Bith inside. Endril waited in the background watching the crowd mill restlessly in the street.

A trumpet sounded, far off, and the thunder of many hooves could be felt. Soon a hundred armored horsemen clopped noisily down the street, pushing the crowd before them. An elaborate black coach, pulled by a team of sweating draft horses, was in their midst and came to a halt in front of the building. Moments later a group of men emerged on a balcony high above the street and one of them read a proclamation.

"Citizens of Baoancaster! The lord mayor in his wisdom, and on the advice of the council, has decided that the witch is too dangerous to hold in this town. The wicked creature will therefore be transported to the tower of the great wizard, Murcroft, who has graciously offered us his assistance. There she will be kept under lock and key, and under his magic powers, and will, as a consequence, be unable to practice any more of her vile black arts!''

What remained of the angry mob was not happy with this announcement. A few cheered, others grumbled, and then realizing that there would be no further excitement, began to disperse. Endril whistled quietly. This was getting more complicated by the minute.

The door to the stone building burst open again, and a coterie of soldiers rushed Bith into the waiting coach. Orders were barked and the coach and its entourage of armored riders were off with a clatter. The procession rode swiftly down the street, around the corner and vanished into the night.

The steady bounce and lurch of the coach was making Bith sick, and she could not move her arms to steady herself. What was happening? Elizebith opened one eye and tried to steady her aching head. The night had become a blur since the moment the soldiers first seized her. Now the air was thick and odorous, and it was difficult to breathe. She was seated between two large men, and her arms were chained to either side behind them. In the dim light she could make out three others seated across from her, talking in low voices.

One of them noticed that she was awake. ''Ah, my sweet. I see that you have decided to rejoin the world of the living for a while.'' He reached across and tweaked her chin. All she could do was moan. ''Not feeling too good, are we. Nice uncle Murcroft will soon fix you up,'' he said with an evil laugh, which was quickly taken up by the others in the coach. "I have had my best room appointed and made ready for you, my dear."

The words made little sense to her. The queasiness in her head was overwhelming and Bith could stand it no longer. A terrific bump sent her stomach into fits. She moaned, and unable to control herself, emptied the contents of her stomach into the man's lap.

The coach screeched to a halt and from the depths of her misery, Bith was vaguely aware of a good deal of shouting and cursing. Then they were moving again and she tried to think of ways to escape. She was bound hand and foot. She couldn't reach her belt . . . and she was sick, tired, and dizzy. Unable to sustain the pain of consciousness, Bith fell into a fitful sleep.

She awoke a short time later to find herself in the iron grip of two large men who were dragging her up a long stone stairway. It wound steadily upward in a long, seemingly endless spiral. Now the steps had turned to wood, and their footsteps echoed off the stone walls. Round and round they went, up and up, and up. It made her woozy again. The men stopped at a rusty iron door, which squeaked ominously as they pushed it open.

Bith was dragged into a dark place and dropped unceremoniously onto a pile of straw. The iron door squeaked shut with a loud clang, eliminating all light. The room was now pitch black. Bith rolled over in the straw and began to sob piteously.

Ormoc, who had been watching through his crystal, leaned back in his chair. There was a tear in his eye.

"What have I done to her?" He sat sadly in the darkness with his arms folded, feeling powerless in the relentless grip of the evil Schlein.

• • •

Hathor slouched down into the chair, rubbing his aching head while he ran his fingers through the tangled thicket of his red hair. The dwarf paced nervously back and forth, mumbling rhymes to himself, while Endril dunked Cal's head repeatedly into a tub of cold water.

"*Gurgle, splut, aach!* Enough, Endril! Enough, I'm all right!" protested Cal. The elf released his grip and the boy threw a towel over his face and groaned miserably. "Why does the worst crisis come when I have a hangover?" He stood up straight at last and looked at the others. "Well, what are we going to do?"

"Rescue her, of course!" snapped Hathor testily. "It all our fault she in trouble!"

Endril put his hand on the troll's shoulder to calm him. "It's not a question of *what* we will do. Our task is clear— rescue Bith. The problem is *how* to accomplish the task."

"Curse us for getting so drunk!" wailed Cal. "We could have saved her."

The elf shook his head. "No, even if you had been sober there was nothing you could have done. That was a carefully planned operation. The soldiers went straight for me, and I saw others watching you. They knew who they wanted and who they needed to suppress. Murcroft's involvement makes me think the Dark Lord, or Schlein is behind this."

"Oh, great," complained Cal. "We're up against him again and this time we don't have a Runesword or Bith's magic to help us."

"Well, he doesn't have a host from beyond the Mistwall with him either. . . ." Endril frowned. "At least I hope not. It would not bode well for this fair land if he did."

Gunnar Greybeard stopped mumbling and turned to face the others. "We're going to need horses. It's a long ride to Murcroft's tower. I have enough gold left to hire some! Let's be off!"

Hathor objected, "No horses! Horses not like troll smell!"

"Not to worry, I think I can take care of that. That's the least of our problems," replied the dwarf.

They packed up their belongings and made for the blacksmith. Hathor hid round the corner, to make the transaction easier. Gunnar fast-talked the befuddled smithy into accommodating them for a ridiculously favorable amount and was soon in possession of three fine riding horses, a draft horse for Hathor, and a pony for himself, all with saddles. The dwarf had worked some kind of magic, for all of the animals nuzzled up to the troll.

"Not a bad deal if I do say so myself," clucked the self-satisfied dwarf as they rode out of the town. "Cost me next to nothing!"

"Why the extra horse?" puzzled Cal.

The dwarf turned in his saddle, "For Bith, of course. If you want to succeed at something you must do everything that might possibly help you achieve your goal!"

Endril smiled.

They rode at a good pace, sometimes at the walk, sometimes trotting, throughout the day. The dwarf was soon spinning another yarn, this time a story meant for their mounts as well, a fable about a horse with wings. Swiftly the four plus one, minus one, rode over the hills and through the fields. Before Cal realized what had happened, it was sunset and they were at the edge of the forest that surrounded Murcroft's tower.

The boy complained, "Gunnar, your tale has kept us from discussing what we would do when we got here!"

"Maybe so," replied the dwarf glibly, "but we have also arrived a day early. Let us spend that day scouting about and making our plans."

Endril laughed. "Quickly then," said the elf, "let's get

off the road and into the woods, out of the sight of any watchers.''

They led their mounts into the forest of pines and junipers and were soon walking on a soft bed of needles. Hathor remarked on how pleasant the place smelled. Endril agreed.

''These are goodly trees. I like them,'' said the elf, ''and they return our good will, Hathor.''

The flat ground soon gave way to a series of steep little hills and it was difficult getting the horses up one side and down the other. They had to struggle, pull, push, and cajole each animal, one at a time. When at last they came to a little grassy clearing between the hills, Endril stopped them.

''We'd best camp here, for we shall get these horses no further. See how the land rises sharply from this point on.'' He pointed in the direction of the tower, the top of which was barely visible above the treetops. Cal could see nothing, as it was too dark for human eyes to see, but Hathor and the dwarf nodded in agreement.

Even as the others were tying up the animals, Endril slipped off into the darkness. At the edge of the clearing he called back to his friends, ''I shall return by morning. Make camp and get what rest you can, but set no fires. We're not alone in this wood.''

The wind began to pick up and the air was chill. There was a feel of winter to the night. Cal, Hathor, and Gunnar spread out their blankets under the cover of some junipers and huddled together for warmth. The dwarf opened his pack and produced bread and fruit, and some thick roots for the troll. The three eagerly addressed themselves to the meal.

''By the gods, I haven't eaten all day!'' exclaimed Cal. ''There's another catch to your darn stories, we never stop to eat!''

''Or drink! It saves time, you know,'' said the dwarf with

a chuckle. "Yet I'm certain your stomach will catch up with you. Now, have I told you the one about the queen who sought her nine sons . . . ?"

Schlein stood on the battlement of his castle with his arms folded. He wore a great bearskin cape over his otherwise bare shoulders and torso. The iridescent mist swirled around him as he watched the sky turn from grey to black, which was about as much of a sunset as you got behind the Mistwall. Others might not be able to see through the murky swirling stuff, but Schlein could, even in the dark.

And now he saw what he had been looking for. A deep *thwumping* grew increasingly louder and gusts of wind swept the place where he stood. Suddenly a gigantic black form appeared over the castle. Two massive taloned claws smashed down onto the stone floor, shaking the heavy building to its roots.

The three servants and the orc guards in attendance screamed and fled below in terror. Schlein merely turned and cursed at the new arrival.

"You're late!" bellowed the evil wizard. "I do not like to be kept waiting!"

A great ugly head at the end of a long scaly neck snaked down out of the mist and eyed the man with the golden hair. "It . . . could . . . not . . . be . . . helped!" growled a slow, deep, reptilian voice.

"Well, I've no time to waste," snapped Schlein. "Stop talking and let's be off!"

"As . . . you . . . wish!" came the rumbling reply. Another huge claw came down out of the mist and Schlein climbed into it. The black dragon lifted his master onto his back to the special saddle fitted there. "Are . . . you . . . ready?" asked the reptile.

"Yes, damn you!" came the curt reply. "Now be off!

Fly into the night!'' Schlein's voice echoed off the dark walls. The dragon beat its wings and then they were airborne, surging forward through the blackness in the swirling fog.

Soon they rose above the mists and stars appeared, and the dragon flew even higher. In time they were beyond the Mistwall and the realm of the Dark Lord, flying low over hands yet unconquered, but soon to fall if Schlein could work his will. The wizard leaned from side to side, taking it all in, noting the roads and trails, the farms and the villages. All he surveyed would belong to him and the Mistwall, and all those tiny ants below would call him Exalted Master, ruler of men!

Below, those of the land cried out in terror. Dogs barked wildly, men ran for cover, and mothers screamed and folded their children in their arms as the great black shape blotted out the stars in its passage through the night.

''There are several secret ways that lead into and out of the tower,'' Endril said as he described what he had discovered in his night of exploration. ''That Murcroft is a clever one, if he, indeed, is responsible for all the tunnels. An army that took this place would not have him in its grasp.''

''Bad as Cairngorm?'' asked the troll.

''Almost. The bolt holes are numerous.''

''Well, are there ways we may take?'' demanded Cal.

''Two at least, though I think one is less guarded than the other. That is the one we shall take. There are many orcs and men in these woods, so we must not travel any further by day. While I rest, Hathor, you and Cal fashion two ladders.''

The troll unsheathed his axe. ''No problem!''

''Do it quietly,'' cautioned the elf, ''and make them

twenty feet long. No more, no less. Now, I am tired and need sleep.'' So saying, Endril crawled into the blankets and fell asleep under the cover of the junipers.

"Listen,'' said the dwarf, "you two may not travel by day for fear of discovery.'' Gunnar took off his red hat and stuffed it under his belt. "I, on the other hand, am a master at not being seen. I shall scout the field of our foes and bring back whatever information may be of value to our cause. If I should chance upon anything I will add it to that which we already know, thereby increasing our chances of success. If I am not back by nightfall, go on without me.''

That said, Greybeard tugged on his whiskers and disappeared before their very eyes.

"Well, I never!'' exclaimed Cal.

"Long speech, good trick!'' the troll said admiringly.

The two turned to their task, and by noon had fashioned two sturdy ladders of the prescribed length. They ate a bit of lunch and then Hathor suggested that Cal take a nap till dark, for tonight he would need his strength.

"What about you, Hathor? You may be up all night as well, you know.''

"Hathor sleep too much already,'' came the answer. "Not good for me. You sleep, I watch!''

So Caltus joined Endril, and the troll sat in the bushes, listening, watching, and waiting for night to come.

"You saw them enter the wood?''

"Yes, and they made camp in that little valley yesterday. You can just see it down there among the trees.''

"Do you think they'll come?''

"They've had time to scout. I left the western ways open and unguarded; they must have found them by now, for one of them is an elf.''

"Yes, I know. Ha! Tonight I shall have them all!''

"Quite so, Exalted Master."

The two figures disappeared from the top of the tower.

A thick bank of grey clouds covered the sky, and the setting of the sun made their presence seem even darker and more ominous. Now it was not only cold, but cold and damp. Hathor shook Endril gently, and the elf stirred.

Cal was up already, yawned, and spoke, "So, it's time." He looked around for the dwarf. "Any sign of Gunnar Greybeard?"

"No, not yet!"

"Why? Where did he go?" asked Endril, sitting up quickly, throwing the blankets aside.

"After you went to sleep this morning, he said he was going to do some scouting of his own, and then just vanished!" answered Cal.

"Hmm." The elf scratched his chin. "Strange he should disappear on the eve of this desperate venture."

"He say if he not return, go on alone!" Hathor came to the defense of the strange dwarf he had come to like.

Endril stood up and stretched. "Well, we can't wait for him now. Cal, you make sure the horses are secure. Hathor, hide our stuff under the bushes." Endril picked up one of the ladders and examined it in the dim grey light. "Good work, just what we need."

The three set out as stealthily as they could with two twenty-foot ladders in tow. Endril led the way, followed by Hathor carrying one end of the ladders, and Cal the other. The grouping worked well, as the leaders could see their way in the dark while the boy was effectively blind. They climbed to the top of a ridge and followed it for some time, gaining slowly on the great hill, topped by the massive tower.

The elf then turned left and took them down a loose gravel

slope. Cal lost his footing and tumbled down sideways, clinging tenaciously to his end of the ladders.

"You all right?" whispered the troll.

"Yeah!"

"Quiet!" cautioned Endril.

They came to a stone wall and the elf directed his companions to use their ladders to scale it. By the time they reached the top, they found Endril there waiting for them. They concealed their surprise, and drawing the ladders up behind them, swiftly joined him.

"Do we need these anymore?" whispered Cal, indicating the ladders.

"I'm not sure," came a hushed reply. "We may, once we're inside." Hathor and Cal shouldered their ladders again and followed their guide. Now they were climbing the steep shoulder of the mountain itself, and the going was slow and difficult. Cal was breathless but did not complain. Hathor took it all in stride.

A trail appeared beneath their feet and the ground became level again, and Cal breathed a sigh of relief. Relief that is, until they reached the log. It was over eight feet in diameter and seemed to stretch forever in either direction. Endril was over it in an instant. Hathor and Cal took a little longer. They laid their ladders on the log, then Cal stood on one end while the troll climbed up into the darkness. Suddenly the boy whooshed up into the air as Hathor's weight brought the other end down. Caltus lost his grip and came tumbling down, to land in a heap at the troll's feet.

"Phew!" he whispered, struggling to stand. "You could have warned me!"

They were retrieving their ladders when the voice of Gunnar Greybeard echoed out in the darkness.

"Minum, sinun, Killinuu;
Go back, go back, they've laid a trap for you!"

Endril was beside Cal and Hathor in a flash, urging them,
"Quickly, back up and over!"

There was a lone shout and then hundreds of voices broke
into a war cry in the darkness around them. Robed figures
rushed them from all directions. Cal misstepped and fell off
the ladder. There were hands everywhere, grabbing, reaching, ripping at his clothes. Endril made it halfway up the
great trunk but was seized and pulled back down. Hathor
flailed wildly, tossing his assailants into the air. He went
for his axe, but was bowled over at the knees by a swarm
of attackers and finally subdued.

"We have them!" shouted one of the robed figures.

A familiar evil laugh rang out from somewhere above.

"Good, bring them in and let's have a look at them!"

Endril struggled under the mound of bodies. His arms
were crushed in against his body and he was unable to get
to the dagger or the white glove which was imbued with
magical powers, and invaluable in battle. Wait a minute,
what was this lump in his belt? The wand Bith had dropped
in the tavern! Worth a try. He pulled it free and rolled it in
his fingers. He was not much at magic, at least not Bith's
style of spellcasting, but he did know an elvish trick or two.

Praying that it might be a wand, Endril muttered an in-
cantation he had learned a hundred years ago and not used
since.

The explosion was breathtaking, to say the least. A brilliant flash of white light engulfed the dale. Endril and his
attackers were blown into the air by the force of the blast.
The wand flew out of Endril's hand and began to circle
above them like a flaming skyrocket, screaming and shoot-
ing sparks as it went. The robed assailants were thrown into

confusion. Endril landed next to Cal and Hathor, his fall broken by one of the enemy.

"Up the ladder! Quick, get out of here!" he screamed. The two scrambled up the ladders. In a flash Endril had his white glove on one hand and his dagger in the other. An attacker came at him only to be slapped senseless by the elf's mysterious glove. Another died as he impaled himself on Endril's deadly dagger. Cal and Hathor had scaled the log and yelled for him to follow.

The elf crouched low for the leap and then sprang for the top of the great trunk. Suddenly the tree trunk was no longer a tree trunk. It rolled and began to move. A huge black claw came out of the darkness and grabbed the elf in midair. Endril saw, too late to save himself, that the "log" was a huge black dragon!

"Flee! Save yourselves! Save Elizebith!" he screamed as another claw closed around him and he was silenced.

Cal was thunderstruck at the sight of the claw that had grabbed Endril. The elf's words fell on numb ears. Hathor, however, had heard Endril's directive and grabbed the boy by the arm and dragged him bodily down the trail as fast as he could run. A group of hooded figures were after them in hot pursuit. Suddenly there was Gunnar Greybeard standing in front of them.

"Quick, no time to lose!" the dwarf said excitedly, taking hold of Hathor's pants leg. "Follow me!" He pulled at his beard and the trio vanished.

CHAPTER
6

Elizebith of Morea spent her first night in the tower of Murcroft in tears. She was sick, disoriented, bruised, and hungover, not to mention scared out of her wits. When, at length, she was able to walk, she stumbled fearfully around the blackness in which she had been imprisoned. She smashed into a cold stone wall, and then felt her way around. The place was a rough semicircle with a bulge on the flat side. She bumped her forehead on a place where the roof slanted low, and came to the iron door. Along the far wall she felt a smaller iron fixture, possibly a window.

She tried to cast a light spell, but her mind was fogged and filled with confusion. It was as though she had forgotten how to work a spell. There were no furnishings save for the pile of moldy straw, and she hoped, sincerely, that nothing else was in the room with her. At last Bith crawled back to the pile of straw, curled up into a ball, and tried to sleep.

When she awoke, there was a thin line of light shining through the iron fixture she presumed to be a window. Bith explored the aperture, feeling, prodding, pulling at anything that felt like a knob or latch. Something gave, and to her relief, the metal door swung open. The blinding light of day shone in her face and she put her arm in front of her silvery eyes to let them adjust.

Behind the door were thick iron bars set in the stone. It was obvious that she was quite high and her cell looked down on a forest below. Then the name of Murcroft came to her and she knew instantly that she was his prisoner. Then another horrible thought came to her. Clement had said Murcroft had dealings with the Dark Lord. The reward on her head! Schlein!

In the light of day, Bith meticulously examined her belt and its contents. Everything was still there with the single exception of the silver wand. Bith wondered what had happened to it. Well, it was time now to do something about her predicament. What would be the appropriate spell? Finally she decided to try to blast her way out the window and float down to the forest below. She reached into a pouch for some powder . . . which pouch was it now? Or did she need these leaves? How odd. Now why would she forget something as simple as that? Bith shook her head and tried again and again and again. Nothing she found was right for the spell. Or was that the spell she wanted to use? Confusion overwhelmed her and she sat down under the window, discouraged.

Just then there came a rap on the iron door. A small slot near the floor opened and a plate and cup were thrust inside. Bith jumped to her feet and ran to the opening.

"Wait, don't go! Who are you?" she yelled. Bith flung herself at the small door, but it slammed shut before she could reach it, leaving her with bruised knees and elbows that added to her anguish.

After her tears were exhausted she rolled over to see what had been given her. On the tin plate was but a single thin slice of bread, and the cup held naught but a draught of murky water.

Bith carried her meager meal over to the window and sat disconsolately on the ledge. She stared out over the forest thinking of Endril, Cal, and Hathor . . . surely they would come for her. They would find a way to get her out of here. Bith slowly tore little bits off the slice of bread and nibbled on them, not wanting to think what would become of her.

All efforts she made to remember and cast her spells came to naught. The words fled from her mind and she couldn't find the material components in the pouches of her yellow belt. Elizebith became thoroughly disheartened.

The next morning the sky was cloudy and the air was cold. Shivering, she dragged her pile of straw over by the window and made a nest in the dim light. The bread and water arrived, and once again she was unable to catch or speak to whomever brought it. She heaped up a small pile of straw and tried to set it on fire with magic. She had forgotten what to do or say. Bith cursed out loud. Somebody or something must have cast a powerful spell over her, for it was obvious that her abilities as a sorceress were currently nil.

Just before dark Bith heard the heavy tramp of many footsteps coming and going on the stair beyond the iron door. Something out of the ordinary was taking place. Bith put her ear to the food slot and listened. Men spoke of the fight, the attack, the dragon. What did it mean? She hoped it had something to do with her rescue.

That night, she awoke with a start. Terror filled her heart, and Bith was certain she had heard the voice of Schlein. Then there was an explosion outside. The room was filled with a flash of white light. The girl jumped to her feet and looked down into the forest. Could this be it? Were her companions coming to rescue her? Something strange, in-

deed, was going on down there. Shadows danced back and
forth in the odd light, figures milled about amid the fireworks.

Soon the fireworks ended, and she could hear voices
shouting from all over the woods. She leaned against the
bars and watched, and waited, and hoped. The woods had
fallen silent and she had not been rescued. A cold wind
whipped against her cheek, and Bith became aware that she
was shivering. She burrowed into her pile of straw, burying
herself in its stink, and cried herself to sleep once again.

"What do you mean, they escaped?" the Exalted Master
bellowed across the room at the three figures who cowered
against the door. "You told me you had them!"

"We did have them, Master, but they had powerful
magic," pleaded Murcroft. "More powerful than mine! The
dragon tried to follow their scent, and even it could not find
them!"

"But we did get the elf!" blurted the robed warrior who
stood beside Murcroft. "We have him in irons."

Schlein arose from his chair before the fire and advanced
on the three, the gold jewelry on his chest glittering in the
firelight. The men pressed themselves against the unmoving
door. Then, to their amazement, their master slapped his
hands on his hips and the oversized face of the tyrant twisted
into a toothy grin.

"You're lucky I'm in a good mood tonight!" Schlein
stopped beside a table laid with food and wine. "Those
fools will keep coming back as long as I have the girl."
He put a large bottle of wine to his mouth, emptied it in a
single gulp, and then smacked his lips. "We'll take them
one at a time if we have to! Come, have some food and
drink!"

Murcroft was the only one brave enough to join Schlein

at the table. The other two stayed back and the warrior called from the door.

"What would you have us do with the elf, Exalted Master?"

Schlein waved his big hand as though it mattered little. He picked up a haunch of roast meat and bit into it, ripping out a huge chunk. He spoke with his mouth full, "Throw him in your dungeon!" Bits of food spilled down his chin and rolled off his belly.

"And summon Ormoc, my scryer!"

The men at the door disappeared, glad to be away from Schlein's evil presence. Minutes later, there was a timid knock at the door. Ormoc, his robes and hair somewhat in disarray, stood with his crystal in his hands.

"Ah, scryer!" boomed Schlein, "I have another small job for you. Those companions of Elizebith . . . two of them escaped tonight thanks to our host's incompetence." Murcroft choked on his wine and Schlein threw the wizard an evil glance. "I want you to find them and keep an eye on what they're up to. Give your reports to Murcroft. When they return for the girl, we shall be ready for them!"

Endril felt the second cold, black claw close around him, crushing the breath from his lungs, and then he lost consciousness. When he regained his senses, he was lying on the ground with chains binding his hands and feet, his dagger and magic glove gone. Three robed men with torches stood over him. He struggled against his bonds.

"So, you live! So much the worse for you," one of the figures said gruffly. "Better the black dragon had killed you," another snarled. The third was silent but kicked Endril in the back.

"Up on your feet, dog! We got better things to do than be yer keepers."

As the elf struggled to stand, one of the robed men grabbed his tunic and jerked him to his feet. A sharp object pricked his back and Endril stumbled forward, his feet hobbled together, as they led him into a black tunnel in the side of the hill. This was not one of the holes he had explored, but quite similar.

The way wound first to the right, then left, and abruptly down. So steep was their descent that the elf stumbled on his chains and bowled over the man in the lead. After a beating, he was righted and they pushed on mercilessly.

At length, they stayed the march, and one of the robed men produced a set of jingling keys. A door was opened and they pushed their prisoner into a smoky, torchlit room, hewn out of the rock of the mountain. Three pig-faced orcs jumped to their feet and scurried for their weapons.

"Put this one away!" ordered one of the men, as he shoved Endril forward. "And mind he doesn't escape . . . This one belongs to the Master himself!"

The orcs babbled something unintelligible and then were all over Endril, dragging him across the smelly chamber. There was a squeak and the slam of a door and the men were gone. The orcs dragged the elf to one side and into a low dank hall lined with cells. The moans and wails of the prisoners filled the corridor.

"Water! Lemme out! Food!"

Another set of keys jingled, and another low door was pulled open. The elf had to double over to fit through. When he was halfway through, one of the orcs kicked him from behind, and Endril tumbled headfirst into the darkness of his prison. The jailors laughed uproariously and slammed the door behind him.

After Greybeard grabbed his pants leg, the night became a blur to Hathor. Trees whizzed by at fantastic speed, and though he was just running, he knew that he was not running *that* fast! His feet never missed a step, even when there were roots and rocks in his way. Cal ran at his side, matching him pace for pace, and the little legs of the dwarf were moving so fast they were but a blur.

In a single bound, they leaped the wall that had required ladders to scale only a short time before. Down a slope and up the gravel slide, then along the top of the ridge and then they were back in their camp. The whirlwind run came to an end and the three stood, breathless, in the clearing.

"Puff, pant, gasp, wheeze! Get your . . . puff, huff, puff . . . things!" ordered the dwarf. Hathor dove under the juniper bushes, gathered the blankets and packs and returned in a jiffy.

"We ride horses now?" asked the troll.

"No time. We can't use them in these woods anyway! They're still after us, C'mon!" And once again the dwarf took off into the night, with Hathor and Caltus at his heels. Again the trees sped by. Now they were out racing across a furrowed field. A village flashed by. Then a series of hills.

The breathless escape ended at the mouth of a small cave hidden in a densely wooded valley beside a roaring stream. The three of them collapsed in the soft loam of the darkened cavern. Hathor lay there panting until sleep overcame him.

The troll's eyes crept open as the first light of a cloudy grey morning made its way into the cave mouth. Cal still snored, but Gunnar was busy sorting through the bundles the troll had lugged with him the night before. The dwarf noticed him and proffered a thick root.

"Good morning, Hathor!"

The troll sat up, took the offering and began to crunch. "Morning yes, but not good!"

The dwarf's normally cheerful face was set in a sad expression. "Yes, you're quite right!" Gunnar shook his head and spoke again, quietly, almost to himself, "I'm certainly botching everything. One by one losing them all to the Dark Lord–"

"What?" asked the troll.

"Oh . . . oh, nothing. Just unhappy at our recent misfortunes."

Cal was up, and rubbed a sore arm, injured in the struggle the night before.

"Gunnar Greybeard," said Hathor, pointing the carrot-shaped root at the dwarf.

"Yes?"

"You magic, why you not rescue Bith? Save Endril?" He bit into the root with a loud crunch.

"Yes, I know magic. But many things are beyond my abilities," lamented Greybeard. "Popping in and out of places unseen is my specialty . . . and bringing good luck, and playing little tricks that fool the eye and ear. And I can forge a mighty blade as well you know." He paused wistfully, "If only we had Sjonbrand here . . . but I am not a fighter and Murcroft and Schlein are very powerful. More powerful than the craft of one small dwarf."

Gunnar broke into a rhyme that made no sense to Hathor, so the troll walked over to the stream and threw some water on his face. Cal came up and stood beside him, bewildered.

"What will we do now, Thor?"

"Don't know . . . Don't know."

The dwarf came crunching over through the gravel waving his finger in the air.

"I have the answer!" he exclaimed triumphantly. "In fact, it is the only answer. I don't know why I did not think of it sooner."

"What, tell us!" demanded Cal.

"Come with me to Northunderland! Caltus Talienson, you shall take Sjonbrand, the Skryling's blade, and bring it here. There's power enough in that mighty sword to bring down all the wizards in that crooked tower.''

Cal scratched his chin, thinking. Hathor said nothing.

"Look, I do not have the power to save your Bith, or the elf. Neither do you two. There were five of us, then four, and now we are three. Do we keep attacking the tower until we are all captured by Schlein? With Sjonbrand in your hands, Cal, it will be no contest. Do you not recall how it felt to wield the Runesword at Cairngorm?"

The heady feeling rushed through Cal, and his face flushed. Never in his life had he experienced such a sensation of godliness. The exaltation, the wisdom, the power . . . he had been untouchable, unstoppable, invincible. Oh, yes, he should like to possess a sword like that again!

"How far away is this place? How long would it take?"

Gunnar was grinning from ear to ear. "Two weeks, maybe three!"

"Phew!" Cal whistled.

"Take too long!" added the troll.

The dwarf put his hands on his hips and paced to and fro for a time.

"I tell you what I'll do. I'll do my now-you-see-me-now-you-don't trick over at the tower and see if I can find out what they plan to do with our friends."

Before anyone could answer, the dwarf tugged at his beard and was gone.

"Hasty fellow," murmured Hathor.

The two spent the morning putting their gear, and that of their missing companions, in order. Hathor organized Endril's things, and Cal sadly went through Bith's bag, carefully folding and packing her few clothes and belongings. He put a scarf to his nose, closed his eyes and breathed deeply. Her faint sweet scent still lingered. Cal hadn't realized how much he liked Bith—maybe even loved her. Until she was gone.

After the packs were done, Hathor borrowed Cal's stone and sharpened his axe. When the troll finished, the boy took the stone and honed the blade of his sword.

They soon ran out of things to do and began pacing nervously, wondering when and, later, if the dwarf would return. Then, to their astonishment, a little gust of wind hit their faces and there was Gunnar Greybeard standing between them with his red cap awry, and his cloak still flapping. In his hands, the dwarf clutched a rolled-up piece of parchment.

"Sorry I took so long, but getting this wasn't easy, and the guards were most uncooperative!"

The dwarf unrolled the crackly document, squinted a couple times, and began to read out loud, skipping over most of the excess verbiage.

"Now, it says here that the . . . mumble, mumble, 'witch' of Baoancaster, who . . . mumble, mumble, mumble, shall be brought forth at the hour of midnight to be burned at the stake on the eve of the next full moon . . . mumble, in ye full and public view!"

Cal's jaw fell open. "Burned at the stake?"

"That's what it says. Right here in black and brown." Greybeard poked at the parchment with a stubby finger and rattled the document for effect.

Hathor scratched his head, and then counted on his fingers. "Next moon . . . twenty-five days!"

"Burned at the stake," Cal repeated incredulously.

"Plenty of time to reach Northunderland, obtain the sword and return!" said the dwarf.

"What about Endril?" asked the troll, "He alive? Do they burn him too?"

"Well, I couldn't find out much about Endril, but he is

still alive, squirreled away down in the lowest of their dungeons. They probably intend to leave him there to rot forever . . . Which gives us plenty of time to save him.''

Cal sat down on a rock, deep in thought.

''The facts are clear, young man. Your girl is going to burn, and your elf is going to rot in a smelly dungeon for the rest of his life unless you show some courage and some sense. Get up off your duff and follow me to Northunderland. Without Sjonbrand there is no hope.''

The boy stood up at last, doubt still clouding his eyes. ''But if we don't get back in time . . .''

''You forget who you'll be traveling with!'' The dwarf winked and snapped his fingers. ''I have many tales as yet untold, and not a few tricks and charms as yet unused.''

''Are you with me, Hathor?''

The troll nodded solemnly. ''We go!''

CHAPTER
7

The man watched Bith crying in the darkness. He saw her attempt to cast her spells and fail. He watched her nibble disinterestedly at her bread and turn up her dainty nose at the water. He was there when she buried herself in the malodorous straw pile.

Ormoc had seen enough. It pained him to have this lovely girl, his secret love, being treated so. There must be something he could do to ease her suffering. But what could be done that would not attract the attention of Murcroft or Schlein? It was late . . . The scryer left his room and descended the long spiral stair deep in thought.

The next morning, the chief cook in the tower of Murcroft berated his helpers and threw one hapless orc out of the kitchen for stealing two roast hens from the fire pit.

Caltus Talienson stood with his pack on his back and a walking stick in his hand. Hathor stood next to him, similarly loaded. Gunnar was standing on a rock, chanting another rhyme in a tongue that neither understood.

"I wonder what it means," said the boy.

"Not know!" answered the troll with his usual eloquence, "Cast spell, maybe."

The dwarf turned to them, "Well now, ready to go?"

"Not quite," said Cal. "I was just thinking we ought to let Bith know that we haven't forgotten her. You were able to charm those horses the other day. Couldn't you work some of your magic and talk a bird or a bat or something into taking a message to Bith and Endril? Something to tell them not to lose hope."

"That we not quit till they safe!" added the troll.

Gunnar tilted his head to one side, thoughtfully. "Not a bad idea." He hopped down from the rock. "But animals can't talk, I'll have to write a little note for each of them. And no bird is going to get to Endril. We'll have to think of something else."

"A snake could slither through bars," suggested the boy. "And a black one at night would be hard to see."

"Rats!" exclaimed the troll. Cal looked at his companion strangely, then understood.

"Rats know dungeons," he continued, "secret ways, nobody notice rat!"

"Great idea, Hathor. A rat it shall be! Now let me write out the notes and then we can find our couriers. Cal, I'm going to need two lengths of thread!"

The dwarf took out the parchment that announced Bith's impending doom and tore off two small pieces. He rummaged through his pack, produced a small phial of black ink and a long goose quill, and began to write. How the feather came out of the pack unbroken was a mystery to the others. They looked at each other and shook their heads.

With the notes written, the dwarf wandered into the cave a short distance and made a series of clicking and squeaking sounds and then spoke in a high voice:

"Yshkin, viere eloihin.
Come forth from whence you dwell.
Minum, sinum Kallihin.
Seek and find darkness beneath the well.''

Moments later several dark shapes skittered out of the back of the cave and gathered at Greybeard's feet. The dwarf then bent over and picked up an exceptionally large black rat with bright, intelligent eyes.

"You're the one!" he exclaimed, and proceeded to tie the bit of parchment to the animal's tail. That done, he placed the rodent on the cave floor and admonished it in plain language to run swift and true under cover of darkness to deliver the message. The dwarf then spoke again in an odd series of clicks and chirps, and the rat and its fellows were gone.

"One done! One to go!" he said, smiling, rubbing his small hands together.

Greybeard led Cal and Hathor out of the cave and up the side of the valley. He stopped at a thicket of bramble bushes and began to warble like a songbird. The dwarf recited yet another strange rhyme, and several brown birds flew out of the brush, twittered nervously and landed on his outstretched arm.

"You are chosen!" he said softly to one of them, and tied the other note to its foot. Greybeard warbled a bit and sent the birds flying, admonishing them to fly straight and true to the maiden with silver eyes. The tiny flock disappeared into the pale morning sky.

"Now, we must be on our way," proclaimed the dwarf. "There's a tide to catch on the eastern shore."

This time Cal and Hathor had eaten heartily, knowing full well that there would be no more food or drink till Gunnar stopped for the night. The dwarf led them down the

hill and broke into the tale of the witch who stole the sun
and the moon. Soon the world was but a blur of color as
the trio raced across the land. Baoancaster came and went,
unnoticed, and then they were on the Great West Road,
traveling east.

The light of a clear blue day shone in between the thick
bars in the window and the girl huddled in the straw began
to stir. Elizebith was stiff, hungry and thirsty, and chilled
to the bone. She struggled groggily to her feet and contem-
plated the untouched cup of murky water.

"Eeuch!" she said out loud, grabbing the cup angrily.
Bith almost tossed it out the window, but her dry lips and
throat caused her to think twice. Gingerly she put the cup
back on the window ledge. Sooner or later she would need
to drink, no matter how repulsive it now seemed. She began
to dance around the tiny room, slapping her arms and rubbing them vigorously in an effort to warm herself.

Eventually, Bith's efforts brought her to the door, and
she suddenly stopped short. There on the floor was a silver
plate, with two roast chickens and a small loaf of bread.
Beside the plate was a large crystal goblet filled with clear
water. Bith dropped to her knees and there she found a note
which read:

> Do not be seen with this. Hide from watchful eyes!
> Eat in good health. —a friend

Bith glanced around the room nervously. Watchful eyes.
What did that mean? At the moment she didn't care. She
anxiously snatched up the plate and glass and dashed over
to the far corner of the room where the ceiling came down
low to the floor, and sat down, hoping the "watchful eyes"
could not see her here.

Bith put the goblet to her lips and drank greedily, then tore into the unexpected feast as though it had been weeks since she had eaten last. When there was nothing left but a pile of clean bones, the girl leaned back against the wall, drank the last of her water, and let out a long sigh.

"Thank you, friend. Whoever you are!"

"You're welcome, princess." Ormoc spoke, unheard, to the figure in the mist above his crystal, satisfied with his first real defiance of Schlein.

Murcroft spurred his great black horse to the top of the hill and searched the grassy meadow below him. His two companions trotted up behind and stopped by his side. Dark shapes were dashing about in the grass in a seemingly aimless manner. Suddenly a quail darted into the sky, flushed by one of the orcs. The wizard pulled the hood from the eyes of the falcon and lifted the bird to the sky.

"Kill, my beauty!"

The bird was gone in a flurry of beating wings, darting swiftly toward the hapless quail. The hawk flew in a straight line, gained altitude and then dove suddenly, disappearing behind a hillock. Seconds went by, and Murcroft grew nervous.

"Can you see her anywhere, Stockwood?" asked the wizard, standing in his stirrups for a better view.

"No, my lord. But she has only . . . Ho! There she comes, over there, by those trees, and she has something in her grip!"

The hawk winged its way back to its master and landed deftly with one foot on his gloved arm, its prey held securely in the other talon.

"What have you brought me, my beauty," cooed Murcroft, coaxing a limp animal from the hawk's cruel grip. "What's this? Gurr! A sparrow!" He tossed the small bleeding body into the tall grass, put the hood on his huntress and rode on. He had not seen the bit of parchment tied to the left leg of the wounded creature.

As the three men rode away, several small brown birds appeared in the sky and landed by their fallen comrade, who still moved, albeit slowly. They stayed with her as she struggled to her feet and hopped feebly to the shelter of a low bush.

Gunnar Greybeard ended his tale, as usual just as the sun was setting. They found themselves in a quiet pasture over-looking a small village, where the lights of houses shone warmly in the blue-grey mists of the chilly evening. Cal dug in his pack for a blanket and threw it around his shoulders. Hathor merely pulled his bearskin tighter.

"Why can't we stay down there, snug in a warm house or inn?" asked Cal.

"Kultani kallihin! Our journey is most secret! There are those who watch. Better we keep to ourselves a bit longer." The dwarf produced a bottle of wine from his tiny pack. "This will warm us up!"

They made a snug camp under a haystack and shared the wine. There was still food in the food bag, and despite their great breakfast, Cal and Hathor were famished and devoured a goodly amount. Even Gunnar ate a great deal.

"How much farther to the sea?" asked the boy, for his knowledge of geography was not great.

"Fourscore leagues to the east lies our goal! About as far as we came today!" said the dwarf calmly, as he gnawed on a slab of dried beef.

"We came that far today?" exclaimed Cal.

"I could have taken us farther," answered the dwarf. "But now we have split the distance in twain . . . and I was a bit tired, myself."

"Gunnar, with you along, an army would need no horse-men!" laughed the boy warrior.

"That I have been told! Here, have some more wine."

They passed the bottle round many times. Hathor could not help but notice that its level had not dropped.

"Where I get bottle like this?" he asked.

"They are not easy to come by, but I'll tell you what. When we have completed our quest, you may have this one, my good troll!"

For once the dwarf told no tales of the northland, and when Hathor and the boy had fallen asleep on their blankets, Gunnar Greybeard put the bottle away, and walked out into the field to stare up at the waning moon.

"Twenty-four days to go!" he whispered quietly. "Keep them safe till we return!" He broke into a long rhyme and chanted softly into the night.

The dawn came grey and pale and they could not see the rising sun as the air was heavy with fog, even on their hilltop. They went slowly at first, and it was some time before Gunnar spoke at all, and then he seemed troubled.

"What wrong, Mr. Greybeard?" asked the troll.

"Nothing, nothing serious. Just something a little bird told me. But there is naught we can do but go on. Here now, we've hiked a good mile and I haven't said a word. Let's see, a foggy day is a good day for the tale of the Princess and the Sea God."

Again time stood still, and the road became a grey blur as they hiked swiftly forward through the morning mists. At one point, Hathor could not remember exactly when, the sun came out in all its glory, but it went nearly unnoticed by the speeding travelers. The land was lower now and they found themselves on a broad flat plain. More villages sped by, and Cal saw the spires of a great city which the dwarf carefully skirted, go by in the distance.

". . . and so the Sea God, who had turned himself into a needle, leapt at the young prince. But the prince turned aside, and the needle buried itself deep in the side of the great oak tree. The tree at once turned brown and its leaves fell to the ground, but the needle was held fast. The spell broken, the princess awoke and rubbed her eyes. The Sea God was buried in the tree and she had forgotten him. The prince took her back to his castle and they lived happily ever after!" concluded the dwarf with a grand flourish.

Hathor clapped his big hands. He had enjoyed this tale of love and woe more than any told so far. Cal was smiling too, but his attention turned quickly to their surroundings. The smell of salt and sea was in the air, gulls squawked in the distance, and the westering sun had turned the fields behind them a golden red haze. A mist blew off the ocean and across the land. A small fishing village nestled comfortably next to the ocean not far ahead in the rolling mists of evening. Cal looked at it wistfully.

Greybeard saw the look in Cal's eyes. "No," said the dwarf, "we must not go there. Let our departure go unseen and unheard under the cover of darkness. The Dark Lord has eyes that can see far, and ears that wait for an idle tongue to slip."

He led them off the road and down along a hedgerow. They climbed over a stone fence and crossed a field of stubble, then a low, grass-covered dune, and found themselves on a quiet, sandy beach. Moonlight danced and twinkled in the waves as they washed quietly ashore in a necklace of silver foam. Hathor stopped to admire the lovely scene.

"C'mon, no time to waste. The tide will soon be right!" called the dwarf when he noticed that his companions had paused some distance behind him. They continued along the beach till they came to a place where three small fishing boats lay drawn up on the sand, and stopped.

Cal frowned and surveyed the boats that lay canted on the sand. "These craft are too small to travel the open sea. Surely, Gunnar, you don't intend for us to go out in one of these little things!"

Hathor looked at the puny little boats and clicked his tongue, then walked over and lifted one up with one hand.

"Too small! I not go!" He dropped the boat back into the sand and it cracked and broke in two with a loud snap.

"Gentle fellows, boon companions, have you no faith or vision?" said the dwarf, smiling. "This is Gunnar Greybeard you talk to now!" He pulled a pouch out from under his grey cloak and undid the string.

Greybeard spoke reverently, "This was given to me by my master!" Out of the pouch he pulled a tiny golden boat that seemed almost to glow in the moonlight. The dwarf walked down the lapping waves and placed it in the sea.

Instantly the tiny boat grew in size, and in no time at all, a magnificent longship was floating in the water before them, its sides lined with round shields, with two banks of sturdy oars reaching out on either side. The prow was a meticulously carved snarling dragon whose tail lashed out vengefully at the stern. A tall mast with a furled sail circled gently in the moonlit sky.

"Come, get your feet wet. Climb aboard," clucked Greybeard, with pride.

A little slot high on the iron door slid open and two eyes peered in at Elizebith. She nearly jumped to her feet and rushed to the door, hoping to speak to whoever or whatever it was. But then the malevolent eyes caught hers and a cold terror swept through her body. Those eyes . . . she had gazed into those eyes before.

She rose unwillingly from the pile of straw, entranced, unable to avoid the stare or turn away, and haltingly began to walk to the door. She tried to stop, tried to avert her gaze, but the power of her visitor was too great. Her arms, no longer under her control, reached up and clutched the front of her dress, then ripped it away, exposing her breasts. She heard thick, heavy breathing as she came near the door, still unable to look away or resist the eyes.

Then the little slot banged shut, and she was released. Bith slumped to the floor in tears. She knew now who it was. She had looked into those eyes in the field before Cairngorm. She had made a fool of him . . . even had him under her spell. But now the tables were turned. Schlein had her now. What was he going to do with her?

Bith crawled slowly back to her straw pile and sat, with her knees under her chin, watching the last glow of evening leave the sky, all but overcome with shame and fear. Late in the day, there was another clank and she jumped with terror, but it was only her evening meal of bread and water. Bith rocked herself gently back and forth in the gathering dusk, hoping her "friend" would return with the night.

CHAPTER
8

Endril rolled over on the cold stone floor and with some difficulty, sat up. He was in a roughly hewn room, with a low ceiling. The floor sloped away from the door to a low groove cut along the base of the far wall, where a small stream of water and waste trickled out of one hole, flowed along the wall and disappeared into another small hole on the other side. He glanced to his left and was startled to see a young man with a scraggly beard leaning against the wall, staring at him.

"Hello," said the fellow. "Welcome to the pleasure palace of Murcroft the Magnificent!" The young man crawled over to get a better look at the newcomer. "Me name's John Purkins." He squinted at Endril in the faint light that came in through the small opening in the door. "You be an elf!"

"That I am. An elf called Endril." With a rattle of chains he reached out to Purkins, and the two shook hands.

"Here," said the young man, "I can do something about them chains." He crawled over to a corner and returned with a small file. "Me father were a blacksmith. I had this in me boot when they locked me away."

John Purkins took the elf's hand and began rasping away at the irons.

"What did you do to get thrown down here?" asked Endril, moving back a little to give the young smith more room to work.

"Well, you might say me and Murcroft had a bit of a disagreement. Fer a long time, the ole man got on well enough, then Murcroft starts puttin' on airs. Of a sudden the woods is full of thieves an' even black orcs as should not ought to be in the lands of clean-livin' men." Purkins shifted the file from his right hand to his left.

"Well, one night, six of the wizard's men come to our smithy and wanted six horses without payin'. The ole man, Big George, and me threw 'em out. Later that night they comes back and steals the horses anyways. Next day me old man goes up to the tower to demand his money. Bang! Slam! The ole man's dead. So I got me trusty bow and me best arrow and sat in a tree and waited. Purdy soon that stinkin' wizard rides by and *thwup!* I lets him have it, right in the shoulder. Me finger slipped or I'da killed 'im." The shackle popped loose from Endril's left arm. "There, that was easy!"

"Anyhow, there I was up in the tree with no place to go and all them wizard's men ridin' in a circle around me. I come down a fightin' and put up a purdy good show, but I couldn't whip 'em all, so's they threw me down here for the next hunnerd years or so." The young man paused. "How'd you come to be here, Master Elf?"

"Murcroft has a friend of mine prisoner here somewhere. I was trying to break into the tower, and ran afoul of the black dragon."

"Black dragon? What in blazes is that?"

"A wyrm of dreadful proportions, and I fear, in the service of the Dark Lord. Bleak times are looming over these lands."

Purkins whistled through his teeth. "Well, you done one thing right, I'll warrant. You have definitely broke into the tower now!"

"I think *underneath* it might be more correct." The two smiled at each other.

Purkins worked till his hands grew tired, and Endril took over for a while. A few hours of hard work sufficed to free the elf from his chains. He let out a sigh of relief and stretched out his legs.

"Keep 'em handy," said the young man. He clamped a broken band around Endril's wrist. "Sometimes them orcs takes us out to walk around a little. I put me chains back on like this to fool 'em then."

The seeds of an escape plan had just been planted in the mind of the elf. He asked his fellow prisoner about the habits and personalities of their orc keepers. Purkins knew six orcs by name and several more by their ugly faces, but he advised against escape attempts.

"They marches us out only when there's a whole bunch of them ugly fellows with swords to guard us. Too many to take in a fight."

"We'll just see about that," said Endril quietly. "It just might be possible to get these creatures so busy fighting among themselves that they lose track of what we're up to."

There was a commotion outside. The lock clanked and the door came open slightly. Endril hurriedly slapped his broken chains about his arms and legs, but he needn't have bothered. A battered tin cup flew through the opening, bounced noisily on the floor and landed in front of the elf and his cell mate.

"Here, dog, here's yer doggie bowl!" growled an unseen orc from behind the door, which slammed quickly shut again. John grabbed the cup and handed it to Endril.

"Feeding time! Get up by the door, quick!" Purkins held his cup under the tiny barred window, and a spout poked through and poured out some runny, lumpy stuff. Endril put his cup up and just managed to collect his share.

"Rabbik shtew!" came a gruff voice from outside. "I made ik myzelf. You likes it . . . beeg treet, haw!" The elf looked out and watched a very fat orc waddle out of sight to the next prisoner, and heard the same announcement repeated.

"That be ole Jowls, not so bad as orcs go." The man was devouring the stuff from his cup. "Gives us real food, ole Jowls does!"

Endril wasn't hungry, but sniffed the mixture in his cup. Not unpleasant. Had he known it was to be the best meal he would get there, the elf would have appreciated it more.

Cal splashed into the water, reached up to grab the rail and pulled himself up into the waiting ship. Hathor was next, and the craft tilted dramatically as the weight of the troll made itself felt. Once aboard, the two reached over the side for Greybeard, lofting the dwarf easily onto the deck.

"Thank you both!" said Gunnar with a smile and then snapped his fingers. Both banks of oars began to move as though manned by strong arms and the ship backed away from the beach, out into the bay. Hathor walked along the deck, feeling around where the invisible rowers should have been, but found nothing.

The dwarf snapped his fingers again. One bank of oars dragged in the water, while the others reversed direction and the ship wheeled swiftly around. Soon all oars were again laboring at a respectable pace, and the ship with its three passengers sliced rapidly forward through the moonlit bay toward the open sea.

"Good trick, Gunnar Greybeard," said Hathor as he thumped back to the rear of the ship. "How you do this?"

"Well," answered the dwarf, tilting his head to one side again, "none of this is my doing. This is a very special ship, not unlike the one I told you about in the story. Remember the king's flying ship?"

Cal and Hathor nodded.

"Well, this ship can't fly through the air for the likes of me, but it is very good magic just the same. I have it on a sort of loan, just for this journey. You would be amazed to see how many passengers this ship can carry." Greybeard leaned over and patted the rail lovingly.

"I'm just amazed, period!" stated Cal.

They took off their packs and stowed everything neatly at the base of the mast. Gunnar broke out the food and they quietly sat on the deck eating supper as their proud ship rowed into the night.

They rounded the headland and the craft began to rise and fall with the swell. The wind freshened into a strong breeze. The dwarf grabbed Cal by the arm.

"Watch this!"

The ropes that bound the sail came loose by themselves. Aloft, other ropes squeaked and pulleys groaned and the sail climbed up the mast, flapping noisily at first till it was stretched taut. Then the winds filled it with a bang and the ship jumped forward through the waves. The oars came up out of the water and pulled in with much thumping and stacked themselves neatly along the sides.

A little cheer went up from the passengers. One of them produced a now familiar bottle of wine and some cups.

"A toast," said the dwarf, "to our fine ship, *Skid-bladner*!"

"And to Elizebith," added Cal sadly. "May the gods protect her till our return!"

"Endril too," said the troll.

They brought their cups together with a clink.

After a fitful night's sleep, Bith awoke slowly. She was afraid to look at the door, for fear that her mysterious friend had not come during the night. She sadly examined her torn dress and then brushed the straw out of her hair. When at last she turned to the door, what she saw made her heart skip a beat. She ran excitedly over to her treasures.

There on the floor was a small basin of water and a cloth, a comb and a mirror, a small cushion, another plate of food, a bottle of wine, and some black thread and a needle. There was another note, too, with the same message as before . . . "hide from watchful eyes." This time she had a pretty good idea whose watchful eyes she was to hide from.

Bith gathered the precious items and carried them over to the corner, where she sat on the cushion and enjoyed her meal. That done she took off her clothes and bathed herself. Finally she did her best to repair the ripped dress with the needle and thread. She was not very good at this task, for sewing was not a skill she had learned from her mother.

She sighed. In spite of her mother's teachings, magic could not be listed among her skills either, at least for the moment. A thump at the door startled her and she jumped up, clutching her dress to her body. A roll of parchment had been pushed through the slot. Bith dressed quickly and then examined the new thing.

"Oh, marvelous," she said out loud, after reading what was written on the page. "Now I'm going to be burned at the stake!" She tried to remember the moon as she had last seen it and a sad smile crossed her face. "At least I have a few weeks to live!"

She crumpled the notice of her execution into a ball, threw it on the floor, and stomped back to the corner. Bith picked up her belt and tried once more to bring a spell to mind but could not. She cursed, and spent the rest of the morning untangling her long black hair.

That evening, the slot came open once again, and the eyes peered in, seeking her out. Bith was afraid, but now knew that it was Schlein and was careful not to return the stare. With great force of will she put her arm over her face and slumped down in her pile of straw. She trembled fearfully when she heard his hoarse breath.

The girl waited for what seemed to her an eternity, and then there was a low growl, the slot banged shut, and the evil presence departed. Bith sat up slowly, still terrified, but satisfied that she had scored a very small victory in the war of wills that Schlein waged against her.

Ormoc was troubled. All night he had searched far and wide for the girl's companions. Through his crystal he had been to their camp and examined the ground for footprints, or broken branches . . . any kind of trail. There was none. They had vanished. He searched the inns of the nearby villages one by one, room by room. He went to Baoancaster and checked every corner of the Roasted Swan. No trace.

It was daylight now, and except for his little act of treason on behalf of Elizebith, he had not moved from his seat. He circled as an eagle around the tower in ever larger sweeps, covering the countryside below. Orcs he saw, and farmers in their fields, travelers on the road, brigands in the wood, all manner of beings save those whom he sought.

Ormoc tried one last trick, and cruised rapidly along the Great West Road, back toward the Mistwall, then the North

Road, and the South Road. Finally, he soared beyond
Baoancaster, but he could not imagine what they could be
doing so far away from the tower. Then, as he turned and
began to drift back, he thought he saw a little blur moving
rapidly down the road between some trees, but he blinked
and then it was gone.

Ormoc gave up on the fruitless search and cast his eyes
upon the girl once more. As her image appeared in the blue
mist of his crystal, he marveled once again at her beauty.
She was combing her hair, and looked happier and healthier
than she had the day before. And it was probably true,
thanks to him. He smiled and let the pleasant image fade.

He rose from his chair, and stretched. Now, however, it
was his unfortunate duty to report that he had nothing to
report. Ormoc was quite glad he had to see Murcroft instead
of Schlein, for awful as he was, the wizard was much less
likely to bat him across the room on hearing bad news.

CHAPTER
9

The strong breeze still blew steadily across the deck as a very damp and cold Caltus Talienson shivered into wakefulness. The ship was rearing and plunging, first on her bow and then on her stern, with spray flying across in an almost continuous sheet from the choppy sea. The sky was overcast, and there was little light as the sun was still below the horizon. The boy pulled a soggy blanket around his shoulders and struggled to his feet on the wildly pitching deck. The dwarf was seated next to Hathor at the stern by the steering oar, the two of them huddled below the side in a futile effort to stay dry. Cal stumbled back awkwardly and joined his friends, landing heavily at the dwarf's side.

"Tell me it's not going to be like this the entire voyage!" the boy demanded, only half joking.

"If I could do that I would be a god!" came the reply. "At least we are making wonderful progress. I'll not have to spin any yarns today."

"Tell us story about drought," muttered Hathor.

The wind and sea remained unchanged throughout the entire morning, and finally the dwarf rummaged around until he found a bolt of sail cloth, which the three rigged over the stern to shield themselves from the incessant spray. Inside the makeshift shelter Cal finally managed to dry out a bit and warm up with a meal of bread and meat.

By afternoon the weather had calmed. The spray was gone and the wind and sea were more moderate. Even the sun began to peek out from behind the clouds now and then. Hathor found some fish hooks and line in a little box. Using a piece of one of his roots for bait, the troll threw his hook over the side and waited.

"What do you expect to catch with bait like that, Hathor?" asked Cal sarcastically.

"Fish that like root," said Hathor, smiling. "Fish like root, Hathor like fish. Simple!"

"Except for one thing."

"What that?"

"Fish don't eat roots!" exclaimed Cal.

"We see," the troll said calmly, playing out more line.

"Here, I'll show you how it should be done!" The boy took a hook of his own out of the box, strung it up, then tore off a bit of dried meat from the food bag and skewered it securely before tossing his line over the other side of the ship. "We'll have a contest."

Gunnar Greybeard, having witnessed the forgoing conversation, was not to be outdone. "Mind if I try too?"

"Sure, go ahead," replied Cal. The boy watched incredulously as the dwarf took a line but no hook, tied a small pebble to the end, and tossed it over the stern.

Soon the dwarf's line jerked hard, and Greybeard pulled it in furiously, hand over hand. Over the rail flew a long silvery fish that jumped and bounced on the deck. "That's one . . . a pike, I'd say." He recovered his line from the fish's mouth and cast it back into the sea.

Next Hathor had a bite and pulled in a salmon, orange

beneath and silver on top. "Likes roots," quipped the troll. Greybeard then pulled in a succession of variously shaped fish including some herring, two eels, a tuna, a small shark, and a squid. Cal threw up his hands in defeat and let his line slip over the side.

As the sun went down, the wind gave out, and the oars went back to work. On the horizon appeared a small tree-covered island, and the ship, *Skidbladner,* pulled steadily for the shore. The stars were out in all their glory when they beached, and Hathor jumped out with a line and pulled the craft safely up on shore. The three gathered firewood, and soon had a roaring blaze.

As the day's catch cooked in the fire, Greybeard told of the strangest fish he had ever seen, the dreaded gesnercon. " 'Tis a fearsome thing with an oval body, from out of which spring twelve arms. Eight eyes it has, two in front, two on top, two on bottom, and two in the tail, so you can never sneak up on one. On one end it has the face, mouth, and tusks of a pig, and on the other a deadly snake-like tail with a long fluke on the end." Gunnar paused ominously. "If it ever slaps you on the back with its fluke . . ."

"What happens?" asked Cal anxiously.

"Well then you're likely to wear out your arm, because it likes you and you have to shake all twelve of its hands as a greeting!" Greybeard rolled over backward laughing, and Hathor snickered out loud.

"All right for you, dwarf! First you cheat and use magic in the fishing contest, then sucker me in with a fish tale. I'll have my revenge, yet."

Again they toasted Bith and Endril, and when the fire died down, Hathor kicked it out and the three loaded the remainder of the cooked fish onto the deck and climbed back aboard *Skidbladner*. Once again the ship took charge and rowed them back out onto the moonlit sea.

Two days passed relatively uneventfully, with the ship rowing when the wind was foul and speeding under sail when the breezes blew fair. Gunnar told more tales, and Cal and Hathor had another fishing contest, a "fair" one this time, for the dwarf was excluded. The troll with his roots for bait caught two large tarpon to Cal's single anchovy.

On the third day, as *Skidbladner* was sailing rather close to a small barren island, Cal saw a man on shore waving his arms and hailing desperately.

"Hey, look at that! He must be shipwrecked!"

The dwarf snapped his fingers and the sail came down and the oars went out. The ship changed course and pulled rapidly for the rocky shore. There was no beach, but the man climbed atop a huge boulder, and when their ship came close, he leaped an amazing distance through the air and landed unharmed on the deck with a crash and a jingle of armor.

As the ship backed oars and pulled away from the rocks the newcomer turned to meet the three. He was a thick-limbed man of wide shoulders and huge girth, clad in a fine vest of chain mail, and a silver helm. Round his waist was an intricate golden belt, and from it hung several bags and pouches and some kind of weapon with a wooden handle that extended from a leather case. Most striking of all, however, was his thick red beard and the fine red hair that covered his bare arms and thighs.

The man's face brightened with a smile, and he extended a muscular arm and ham-like hand to Cal. "They call me Red Beard," he said in a deep, pleasant voice, "although others might know me as giant-breaker . . . for I have no love of giants!" Cal shook his hand and introduced the others. The big man avoided all explanation of how he had come to be on the island and although that was odd, the three out of courtesy never asked.

Skidbladner was under sail again, and the transition from rowerless oars to unmanned sails did not go unnoticed by Red Beard, but he said nothing and instead issued a challenge.

"Where I come from we do a lot of wrestling, and there are few who have thrown me. Caltus Talienson, do you think you can best me?"

"I can surely try!" answered the boy. Cal, too, had wrestled and felled many a fellow squire in his days as a soldier. He stepped forward and spread his feet. The two locked arms. Cal flexed his muscles and strained. Much to his alarm, it felt as though he were trying to move a mountain of rock, for no matter how hard he pulled or pushed, Red Beard did not budge an inch. Then, without warning, his opponent gave a quick twist and threw the boy sprawling to the deck.

The big man slapped his hands together merrily. "Well done lad, you have a great future as a warrior!" He turned to the others. "Greybeard, 'twould not be fair for me to wrestle you down, though like as not you'd have some trick up your sleeve for me. You, Hathor, do you think you can best me?"

"I try!"

The two locked arms and Cal and the dwarf backed away, fearing what might happen as a result of this contest. For a minute, the two stood motionless, straining against each other. Hathor let out a grunt and the two jerked slightly, then Red Beard made a similar noise and they wiggled again. It became obvious that the two were pretty evenly matched. Hathor was, after all, noted for his great strength.

Suddenly the contest became animated, and the two began dancing about the deck, still locked together in each other's iron grip. The two wrestlers now grunted and groaned audibly, and even though there was a cool breeze blowing, beads of sweat crossed their brows.

Hathor snarled, revealing his fang-like trollish teeth. Finally, Red Beard jumped back and threw his arms up, breaking the embrace. "It's a draw!" he declared, laughing. He then turned to the others. "You did not tell me your friend was a troll!"

"You didn't ask!" said Gunnar, smiling.

"Haw! Point well taken, Master Greybeard! Well, all this business has given me quite an appetite. Have you any food and drink?"

Red Beard was led to the stern, where Gunnar broke out the food bag, and Hathor brought forth the fish. The four sat down to a hearty meal. Things went well at first, but then Cal noticed a look of distress in the dwarf's eyes as Red Beard consumed everything on the ship, all the fish, both cooked and uncooked, forty loaves of bread from Gunnar's magic bag until no more would come forth, and all the roots that Hathor had not managed to snatch away from the man.

At last Red Beard belched. "And now some drink, ah, is that a bottle of wine I see there?" The big man reached across and grabbed Greybeard's endless bottle of wine.

"Oh, no!" The dwarf put his hands over his eyes and groaned.

Red Beard put the bottle to his lips and the others watched in spellbound horror. The man drank, and drank, and drank. For over an hour he drank, then he paused and wiped his lips with the back of his hand. "Good vintage stuff you have here, Greybeard!"

He put the bottle back to his lips again, this time for a mere half an hour, and then stopped. "Ahhh!" He held an empty bottle in front of him for all to see. Hathor shook his head sadly.

"Very tasty, indeed!" Red Beard placed the bottle carefully on the deck and then stood up to stretch.

"This is fine ship you have here!"

"Yes, we're quite proud of her," answered the dwarf nervously.

Red Beard ran his hands lovingly along the rail. "Good lines, fine craftsmanship. Could it be that I have sailed on her before?"

"Quite possibly, sir, as I only have her on the most temporary of loans. We are on an important quest to Northunderland!"

"A quest, eh? And what might be its nature?"

Cal was standing next to them. "I seek the sword Sjonbrand with which I intend to rescue Elizebith of Morea from the clutches of Schlein, servant of the Dark Lord."

"Sjonbrand!" Red Beard scratched his chin under his whiskers thoughtfully. "Ah, Sjonbrand, forged of Glasvellir?" His eyes brightened.

"The very same," answered the dwarf proudly, holding up a diminutive fist. "Forged of Glasvellir by this very hand . . . and others, of course."

"Well then, that explains all this!" He broke out into a deep cheerful belly laugh, and then walked back to the stern, where a mound of fish bones lay on the deck, the depleted food bag and the empty bottle. "Then I must thank you all for the pleasant company and the fine food and drink."

He pulled the weapon, which they could now see was a hammer, out of the leather sheath in his belt and held it over the site of the feast while reciting a small verse. One moment it was a scene of carnage, the next it was a picture of plenty. Fat fresh fish flipped about on the deck, and the bag bulged once again with food. And what pleased Hathor most of all was the fact that the wine bottle was once again full and corked.

"Now I bid you farewell in your quest for Sjonbrand!" So saying, Red Beard re-sheathed his hammer, dove over the side and disappeared under the waves.

"Kilwch and Olwen!" screamed Cal, running after the man. "He'll drown with all that armor on! Get a rope, we must save him!"

"Calm down, Caltus," said the dwarf calmly. "That fellow is in no danger of drowning. You don't know how lucky we all are to still be here in possession of *Skidbladner* . . . and our throats! That was Thor himself!"

CHAPTER
10

Brightfeather tucked her head under her breast and inspected the parchment and prodded the knotted thread with her beak. Greybeard's note was still tied securely to her leg. She bravely stretched her broken wing and tried a few tentative beats. It pained her greatly, but it was getting better. Soon she would again fly. Here came Flashtail with a beak full of seeds.

"Thank you, good friend," she chirped. There was another flutter of wings and under the bush came Flax Seed and Thistle, the first with a tasty mosquito, the second with a fat fly in her beak, both of which Brightfeather gobbled eagerly.

"Gracious me. If you keep feeding me this well, I shall be too heavy to fly when I am healed."

"I should think not," said Thistle, as gruffly as possible. "You eat like a little butterfly!"

The four twittered noisily at Thistle's remark, and Flashtail made ready to leave. Suddenly there was a high-pitched warning scream from above, and the four birds froze. Whitewing flew noisily over the bush, shouting, "Weasel! Weasel! Beware! Take to the air!"

Her companions were reluctant to leave her, but Brightfeather would have none of it. "Take wing, and save yourselves. I will sit motionless."

The other birds still did not move.

"Go now, I shall be safe! Stealth shall protect me, but if you are killed, who shall feed me?" The wounded bird settled into a pile of dried grass and was barely visible even to the others. Finally, as one, Flashtail, Flax Seed, and Thistle took wing and came rushing out from under the bush and turned abruptly skyward in a fluttering brown blur.

Once airborne, the small flock flew over to Whitewing, who was still circling around the intruder, screaming. It became apparent that the animal was on to a scent, for it was heading relentlessly toward the bush that hid Brightfeather. It would stop to sniff, rise up on its hind legs and eye the four birds in the air, then creep forward, snaking gracefully though the field. The birds had to take action to save their friend.

Thistle went first and landed some distance away from the weasel and began flapping about in the grass as though he was wounded. The intruder stopped and stood up on his hind legs, scrutinizing this new activity. Then, with blinding speed he bounded after the seemingly crippled bird in three great leaps. Just in time, Thistle soared skyward, to avoid capture. The weasel had been turned away from the hiding bush.

Next, Flax Seed flew to ground and pulled the same trick, drawing the enemy still further from it's prey. Flashtail then did the same. By the time Whitewing landed to lure the weasel a fourth time, the creature gave up, ignoring the floundering bird, and departed the field, leaping gracefully over hummocks of tall grass.

For the time being, Brightfeather and her message of hope had been saved.

The black rat, known to his family as See-In-The-Dark and also as Blackwhiskers (the title he preferred), bid farewell to his mother and his brothers and sisters and all of his aunts, uncles, and cousins. He would make the trip alone and unaided, for it would attract less attention. They had many relatives living in the tower, and all present seemed to have one message or another for him to carry to their kin. Blackwhiskers listened patiently to each in turn, doing his best to remember them all.

As the long shadows of evening filled the valley with darkness, a strange procession of rats of all sizes spilled out of the mouth of the cave and followed the edge of the streambed like a long furry snake. The march continued, until the stream passed under a stone bridge. There the escort stayed and Blackwhiskers was on his own. He jumped into the water and swam under the bridge, managing to claw his way onto a mossy bank some distance downstream.

The rat followed the stream most of that night, never once pausing to eat or rest. In the early morning hours, he turned away from the water and crossed a farmer's field, staying always under the cover of a hedgerow. By dawn, Blackwhiskers had reached a small village. He met others of his kind in the refuse heap, and they directed him to the home of a distant relative who lived in the stables.

See-In-The-Dark of Shadowvale Cave was welcomed by the clan of Smith's Stable. They fed him what little there was, for hard times had fallen on the family since the humans had left and taken the horses with them. The place was run down and much to their liking. But the grain on which they had lived so well was now gone, and they were forced to forage nightly in the fields, in order to survive.

Blackwhiskers rested till dusk, and then set out once more for the tower, with still more messages to deliver to friends and relatives of the Smith Stable Clan. He narrowly escaped a mean yellow dog on his way out of the village, and then made his way into the great forest. Again, he went without food or drink until morning found him at the base of the tower by the stream that oozed out of the bowels of the hill.

Three orcs armed with bows stood between Blackwhiskers and his goal, and the scene filled him with fear. Three rats lay dead in the stream, their bodies pierced by wooden shafts. The messenger hid under a tree root and waited.

The orcs were arguing. "Three iz enuff. Lez take 'em in and be done. Damn, itz almost light!" said the first one.

"Grinder wanted five for the stew," complained the second orc. "He'll have our hides if we bring him this puny catch!"

"Grinder can go to blazes! I'm goin' back."

"No, you're not!" The second orc grabbed the first by the throat and was about to punch his opponent in the face.

"Hold it, you two!" yelled the third orc, pulling the others apart. "The dump's on the way back, let's take these and see what we can kill over there before we go in!"

There was much grumbling but finally the three orcs gathered up the slain rats, and skulked noisily off into the morning haze. Blackwhiskers, much relieved at their departure, waited till the big ones were gone and then darted across the open space and disappeared into the cleft in the rock from whence the stream issued.

Once inside, he was immediately greeted by a group of the Blacktails from Under Tower, who were especially concerned about those recently slain. Blackwhiskers then told of his long journey, and of his mission, and delivered some of the messages he had brought from the Cave and the Stable, as well as showing off the important message attached to his tail. This took much time, and each distant relative insisted on talking to him at length, and there were many gatherings and speeches.

By the time all the messages he could remember had been delivered, another day had passed, and he was at last free to continue his quest. A first cousin showed him a secret way and Blackwhiskers anxiously made his way through the rat mazes that honeycombed the mountain.

The meal today had consisted of a chunk of dried bread and a cup of vile broth. Endril had given most of his share to his companion, and was now digging away with the tip of John's file at the wood behind the hinges of the door. It was oak, and very thick, so progress was slow, but Purkins had not even thought of digging out in that manner and was quite enthused. They took turns at the tiresome task.

John yelped suddenly, "Damn, Endril, would you look at the size of that thing! Don't move and I'll kill 'im."

Endril turned quietly. Purkins had his chains in his hand and was stalking a large rat that had crawled in through the drainhole. The rat swished its tail and skittered toward the elf.

"Wait! Don't hurt it!" cried Endril, noticing the parchment tied to the animal's tail.

John was dumbfounded as the rat hopped brazenly into his cell mate's lap, squeaked, and then waved its tail in the elf's face.

"It's a message!" cried Endril, deftly untying the parchment. He rolled it open and held it up to the faint torchlight that filtered in from the hall. "From my friends outside! They have escaped from Murcroft and have gone to fetch Sjonbrand!" He crumpled the parchment as the rat disappeared back the way it had come.

"What's a Sjonbrand?"

"A magic sword." The elf was deep in thought and spoke more to himself than in answer to the question. "If what that crafty dwarf said was true, this is indeed good news." He handed the file to Purkins. "Here, you dig for a while, I must think."

Purkins scratched his head, not really sure what had just taken place, shrugged, and set about his task.

The last few days had been ones that Bith would have liked to forget. Her efforts to revive her magic were constant exercises in frustration and it was beginning to drive her mad. She received her daily ration of bread and water, and each day she was visited by Schlein, who stood at the door and stared at her with clearly evil intent. She had come to dread these visits and was sure he was leading up to something horrible. Had it not been for the food and gifts from her mysterious friend, Bith knew she would be in a miserable state, most likely unable to resist the stares that came at her day after day.

The gifts had been piling up and quite an accumulation of things were hidden around the corner, out of view from the door. She began throwing all her food scraps out the window but there was still a large stack of silver plates, glasses, goblets, cutlery, bowls, pillows, cushions, and blankets. Bith had taken to sleeping in the corner on her cushions and under the blankets, but she made certain that each day when Schlein came, she could be found curled up in the straw. She did not want him to know of her secrets.

One afternoon she was startled to hear keys rattle in the lock and the great iron door swung open. She ran to the corner in desperation, hoping to hide the pile of gifts in some way from whoever or whatever was coming. A high voice called to her.

"Elizebith, daughter of Morea, come forth. You have

been summoned to the presence of the Exalted Master.''
No one entered, so she cautiously crept to the half-open
door and peeked out. There before her stood four men, three
of whom were tall, muscular guards, clad in red breastplates
and leather helms. The fourth was a stooped old man dressed
in a red-and-white-striped robe, and holding a glowing amulet in one hand.

"Come forth, hurry up," urged the old man. "The Exalted Master does not like to be kept waiting!"

Bith slowly slipped out the door. Instantly two of the
soldiers seized her arms and held them together in front of
her. The old man produced a pair of hand irons and locked
them quickly around her wrists.

"There now," he said to the others, "she's safe enough,
I'd say." The stooped man turned and started up the spiral
stairs. The soldiers loomed around Bith and nudged her till
she followed. They climbed a seemingly endless number of
steps, making several circuits of the tower, until at last her
escort halted in front of an ornately carved and painted door.
The old man, still clutching the glowing amulet, gave the
door a push and it swung easily open. "You may go in."
He motioned for her to enter with his free hand.

A cold chill ran up her spine as she started in, for she
could feel Schlein's presence. But there was nothing she
could do with armed guards standing behind her. Inside,
before a roaring fire, sat the awful man. He was seated at
one end of a long table that was piled high with food . . .
roast turkeys, pigs, chickens, ducks, meat pies, bowls of
fruit and great loaves of fresh hot bread. The aroma was
quite delightful, and had she truly been living on bread and
water for the last week, Bith could easily imagine how she
would have reacted.

"Ah, my dear Elizebith." His voice was all sweetness.
"Would you care to join me?" Schlein grinned from ear to

ear and indicated the empty seat opposite him at the table. Bith was sorely tempted. Was it something in the way he said the words? Then she got a grip on her resolve and steeled herself against him.

"No, never!" she cried.

Schlein's eyebrows knotted, his barrel chest puffed up large, and he leaned forward, pointing a huge finger at Bith. "Watch your tongue, Miss! You and I have much to discuss, and that is not the way to address your Exalted Master!" He was looking into her eyes again, the way he had done that first time, and she began to feel true terror.

Bith gritted her teeth, clenched her fists and squinted hard, still meeting his glare. He would not take control of her this time!

Schlein picked up a pair of amber stones from the table and began to roll them between the fingers of one hand. He was silent for a minute, staring intensely at Elizebith in an effort to win her to his will. After a time, realizing that it was not going to work, he shook his head, dropped the stones, and leaned back again, smiling ruefully. "Well, you are a lady of iron will. I'll wager it's a good thing for Murcroft and me that your other powers have been suppressed." He grabbed a glass of wine and drank it down with a gulp.

"But enough of this! You will listen to what I have to say, Elizebith of Morea. You may not like it at first, but I think you will come to see the wisdom in my words as the days pass by." Schlein scooted his chair back with a squeak and rose to his feet, his great bulk seeming to fill the whole room. He walked over to the fire and looked into it, warming his hands.

"A man gets lonely at night, even if he is soon to become a god!" He paused briefly. "You have greater powers than you know. I learned that for myself, the hard way, at Cairn-gorm.''

He turned to face her. "Soon, I will have all the speaking races under my thrall. I will be the God-Emperor. I cannot be denied. But even a God-Emperor needs his Empress.''

Schlein advanced toward her slowly. Bith inched back-ward in horror, but said nothing. She avoided his eyes and stared intently at the gold chains and jewelry that hung on his vast bare chest.

"You will be my bride. You will be my Empress!'' He spoke in a low, excited whisper. His breathing was loud and rapid. Bith backed into the depths of the chair until she could go no further. The giant of a man was now mere inches away. She could smell his body. It was not a man-like odor but something sickeningly sweet . . . and repulsive. She turned her head to one side and stared down at the floor.

Schlein's hands slipped around her waist and Bith let out a yelp. "With your powers allied with mine, with you at my side . . .'' His great fingers reached completely around her slender body and he squeezed her in his hands. The girl groaned with pain and shook her head violently.

"Crush me! Kill me and be done with me,'' she screamed, "but I shall never be yours!''

The angry man lifted Bith up bodily and threw her against the door. The breath was knocked out of her and her head struck hard.

"So you say!'' he snarled. "But you will soon change your mind. Now get out of my sight!'' Schlein turned away from her and went back to the fire.

Gasping for air, Bith staggered out of the room and col-lapsed into the arms of the waiting soldiers.

Ormoc sat in his chambers brooding. Murcroft had just cursed him for the fifth day in a row. His continued failure to find any trace of the girl's companions was beginning to take its toll on him. Murcroft, like Schlein, could be extremely dangerous . . . but it was not as though he hadn't tried. He had spent nearly every waking hour in the search, almost to the detriment of keeping tabs on Bith.

His one consolation was the thought that if he had reported such news to Schlein, he would have been thrown through the stone wall of the tower, into a place where there were no windows or doors. Curse Murcroft and Schlein, anyway.

He now focused his thoughts on Elizebith, and the blue mist appeared. The scryer was alarmed to see Tellarko placing irons on the girl's wrists. That second-rate magician was using his talisman on Bith! Ormoc could see it glow.

Ormoc was even more upset as he watched what went on between Elizebith and Schlein. At first the scryer worried that she might give away the fact that someone had been bringing her food and gifts. But events unfolded rapidly, and Ormoc admired her spirit as she defied the evil one. He pounded his fist against the table when Bith was thrown at the door.

The scryer followed the girl back to her room, and was distressed to see the guards cruelly toss her to the floor just inside the door. He let the image fade and pondered what to do. The princess deserved *a reward* for the way she had handled Schlein. Something to keep her courage up.

Later, in the wee hours, when all was quiet in the tower, Ormoc crept through the darkness, up the winding spiral stair. As usual, the orc guards along the way were asleep at their posts. He came to the carved, painted door and pushed it open. The fire had died to glowing coals, and Schlein was gone. There on the table remained most of the great feast, still untouched.

Ormoc gathered two meat pies, a bowl of fruit, two bottles of wine, and a loaf of bread and then tiptoed back to the door. As an afterthought, he crept back across the room and gathered up the two amber stones Schlein had played with earlier. Maybe they were magic. Back at the door the scryer peeked outside . . . The coast was clear.

Elizebith lay on her cushions, staring into the darkness, determined to be awake when her mysterious friend arrived. In spite of her resolve, she was just dozing off when she heard the telltale clank of the food slot. The girl jumped to her feet and ran to the door. There, in a shaft of dim light from outside, she saw two large pies and a loaf of bread. She dropped to her knees before the door. A hand came through the hole and placed a bottle of wine on the floor, and came back again with yet another bottle.

It was a soft and gentle hand, she thought, and when it entered her prison once more with a bowl of fruit, she reached out and grabbed it. The hand jerked and there was a muffled cry from outside, then it went limp and she clasped it tightly. It was soft, she thought to herself, too large to be that of a woman's, maybe the hand of a prince . . . No, not in this awful place.

The stranger pulled free suddenly, grabbed one of Bith's hands, and drew it through the narrow opening. She felt whiskers and then a gentle kiss on the back of her hand. After a brief pause, two small objects were closed in her palm. Bith pulled her arm back and examined what had been given to her—two strange-looking stones. Without warning the tiny door slid shut.

"No, wait," she cried softly. But Bith heard footsteps on the stairs. Without a word, he was gone.

CHAPTER
11

Hathor, Cal, and Greybeard leaned expectantly over the forward rail, gazing intently at the barely discernible grey mass of land that loomed before them in the early morning fog. The wind had died with the first light and the air was still, cold, and damp. The rhythmic splashes of *Skidbladner*'s oars were the only sounds to break the eerie silence. At last a barren stone hill, jutting out into the sea, came clearly into view.

"That's it!" exclaimed the dwarf, excitedly. "The Point of Doom . . . See the bones." All too visible now were the ghostly remains of many ships, wedged in among the boulders and rocks at the base of the cliff. The ribs of the shipwrecks resembled the skeletons of dead creatures picked clean by vultures. Cal shuddered silently, wishing *Skidbladner* would stay farther out to sea from this dreadful sailor's nightmare.

"Northunderland, friends. We're here at last," said Greybeard with a note of pride in his voice. The dwarf then trotted back to the mast and made his way rapidly up a rope ladder to the top, where he leaned forward and peered anxiously ashore. The ship rounded the headland, leaving the wrecks behind in the mist, and a taller, darker shape loomed ahead of them.

"I'm glad to be past that mess," said Cal.

"Ship go too close to rocks! Hathor glad also." Obviously the troll had felt *Skidbladner*'s passage had cut things a little too close as well.

The ship turned slowly landward now, with the naked cliff barely visible on one side and the dark shape approaching closer on the other. Hathor let out a little grunt of pleasure as the fog lifted somewhat and the looming darkness revealed itself. A dense dark evergreen forest climbed steeply up the slope to their left.

There were sea birds now, and gulls circled above *Skidbladner*, squawking noisily, their calls echoing off the nearby rock face. The sun was up, attempting to burn away the fog that enveloped the travelers. The ship rounded a bend and the gentle rocking of the swell that had followed them in from the open sea left them.

With the mist rising, it became clear that they were entering a long narrow fjord, a sight never before seen by Cal or Hathor, yet familiar thanks to the vivid descriptions in so many of Greybeard's tales. The dwarf broke into a song, whose words the two on deck did not understand, but whose cheerful tone, mingled with the racket from the gulls, raised the spirits of all. Hathor began to whistle through his teeth.

The journey continued most of the morning, with *Skidbladner* turning this way and that, following the tortuous passage between the tree-clad fingers of land that surrounded them. The fog rose and hung above them like a warm grey blanket, trapped in the treetops on the crests of the hills.

A school of porpoises began dancing and dodging with great skill in front of the ship and Cal and Hathor laughed and whistled back as the sea creatures called out their greetings. Then, without warning, their friends in the water disappeared, and *Skidbladner* nosed gently up onto a narrow beach. Instantly, Greybeard was at Cal's side.

"Well, 'tis time we went ashore. We can go no farther by sea!" The dwarf put his hands on the rail and leaped over the side to land in the shallow water with a splash. The others took a bit longer, gathering up their packs, and securing them, before they too jumped down and waded ashore to Northunderland.

The tiny beach ended abruptly in a steep rock cliff which disappeared into the mists above them. Cal looked to either side and saw that they were surrounded by the sheer face. There was no way up.

"Are you sure you want to land here, Gunnar?" asked the boy, skeptically. "There's no way to go but straight up . . . unless, of course, you intend to somehow float the three of us to the top of this slab of rock."

Greybeard chuckled. "No, nothing so fancy. There's a little path that leads up through a cleft in the rock. You'll need me to find it for you! But first . . ."

The dwarf snapped his fingers and *Skidbladner* began to shrink. In a moment it was the size of a tiny toy, and Greybeard lifted it out of the water and carefully returned it to its leather pouch. That done, he shouldered his food bag, took a deep breath and looked cheerfully up at the obstacle before them.

"My, but it is great to be home again. Smell those fir trees!"

All Cal could smell was the dead fish that had washed up on the beach, but he kept silent as Hathor and he trailed behind the dwarf through the sand to the far end of the beach. There, hidden behind some scrubby furzes, was a crack in the rock, and a narrow track led steeply up into the heart of the cliff.

"Stay with me, and watch your step. It gets a bit tricky near the top." The others followed the dwarf as he nimbly hopped and jumped from one rock to another, leading them sharply upward. After climbing for some distance, the crack ended, and Greybeard doubled back along a narrow ledge. They came out again on the face of the cliff, about halfway to the top. Cal looked down, shuddered, and froze in his tracks.

"Oh, by the way, don't look down," the dwarf said calmly, as he disappeared around a bulge in the rock. Hathor stopped behind the boy and nudged him in the ribs.

"You scared?"

"What? Uh, no . . . just stopped to catch my breath." Cal swallowed the lump in his throat and carefully edged along the precarious ledge Greybeard had taken. After what seemed like an eternity, the path widened, and led up a gentle slope away from the cliff and into the clouds of dense fog that hung above the land. Short scrubby trees clung to the bits of turf that filled the cracks in the rock slope, and small yellow flowers peeked out in little clumps here and there along the way.

The mist was so dense Cal could barely see where he was going, and was quite surprised when he bumped into an unseen Greybeard, who had stopped on the trail.

"What is it?" asked Cal. The dwarf was staring at a clump of barely visible trees. Hathor came up and stood beside them.

"The forest of Auseviget," came the hushed reply. "A magic wood. 'Twas here I ran afoul of that awful troll witch, Loviatar, and was changed into a pebble and thrown south. Yet, something's amiss . . ." Greybeard fell silent. Cal could see nothing unusual, and looked to Hathor for an answer. The troll pointed to a small rock cairn by the side of the trail. The whitened bones of a human hand lay at the base of the pile.

The dwarf began to chant to himself:

> "Mina, sina, kuusiken,
> Naelta, Maelta
> Sina, jaat siihen . . ."

Abruptly he turned to the other two. "Well, time's a'wasting, let's be off. And mind you, be polite to any troll women you meet." Greybeard winked at Hathor, strode up the path into the midst of the forest and disappeared into the fog. "This is their territory, you know."

"Troll women?" asked Hathor, hurrying to catch up. The going was somewhat difficult as the trees were now tall and blotted out most of the light, and the fog obscured objects just out of reach.

"The very troll women I told you of in my tales, Hathor. They have lived in these woods for as long as anyone can remember. Tall fair trolls, not unlike you, and most have flaming red hair. Their men are often called to war and their numbers are few . . . at least they were when last I was here."

The three stumbled slowly through fog and forest for some time. Cal stumbled over a tree root and cursed, likening the cloud in which they were traveling to the Mistwall.

"Not same!" argued Hathor. "Mistwall stink. This fog smell good. Clean forest. Pure!"

"Very true, very true," chimed in the dwarf. Then the three stopped in their tracks. Several large pale figures emerged from behind a tree and into their path. The newcomers walked softly forward, and Hathor grunted uncomfortably. They were troll women, every bit as tall and hefty as Hathor, yet strangely beautiful, and they wore nothing save elaborately decorated leather belts slung round their substantial waists. One of them, who held a great battle axe in her hands, recognized the dwarf and smiled, bearing her troll fangs.

"Gunnar Greybeard of Glasvellir Hall! It has been a long time. . . ."

"Lennia, my dear," cooed the dwarf. "I am so pleased to see you."

"Gunnar, much evil has transpired since you disappeared! Where have you been?"

"That, my dear, is a long story, having much to do with your old nemesis, Loviatar."

"Well, rest easy, Greybeard. The witch Loviatar is no more!"

"Good news, indeed—but I am being impolite." The dwarf turned to address Cal and Hathor. "Allow me to introduce my foster mother, Lennia, High Mistress of Auseviget."

She put down her axe and extended her hand first to Cal and then to Hathor. The boy attempted to bow low and stumbled, his eyes fixed on her enormous full breasts. Lennia, however, only had eyes for Hathor, and when he took her hand, she gave him a look that would have melted the heart of the coldest, meanest troll. Thor was speechless.

At length, after the two had reluctantly released their grip on one another, the mistress of the wood introduced her companions. Greybeard invited the troll women to dine, and all sat down under the great pine trees to a lengthy repast, courtesy of the dwarf's bottomless food bag and wine bottle.

In Gunnar's long absence, it seemed, Loviatar had stirred up a great war between the trolls and the giants of Northunderland. All surviving troll males had gone off to war, never to return. The witch had profited, taking the spoils of battle from the ruined halls of the giants.

This went on for weeks until, at last, Lennia could take no more. She raised a force of female troll warriors, tracked Loviatar down and surprised the witch in her sleep. Now the witch was dead and gone, but so too were all the troll men and most of the giants of the land.

"Well, the giants will not be missed, I'm sure," remarked Greybeard. "But it is grave news about your men!"

Lennia had tears on her cheeks, and once again she fixed her eyes longingly on Hathor. The dwarf stood up and put himself between them.

"Lennia, I know what you must be thinking, but Hathor, Cal, and I are on a most important quest." He slapped Thor on his muscular shoulder. "We need these mighty arms at our side, for we must recover Sjonbrand. When that is done, well, I'm certain Hathor could . . ."

As they talked on into the morning, Lennia and the others obviously wanted Hathor, and the dwarf kept steering the conversation away from the troll and back to the whereabouts of the sword. At last Lennia revealed that she had heard that it had last been in the hands of the Skrisung, a warrior tribe of men who lived not far to the east of the forest of Auseviget.

It was all Greybeard could do to pry the troll women away from Hathor, and vice versa, but eventually the company parted, and the four-plus-one-minus-two were on their way again, having made many promises. Promises the dwarf was not really sure he or Hathor would be able to keep.

The forest remained shrouded in mist and fog, and the going was slow and tedious as they wound their way around the low hills and valleys that punctuated the forest. For once Gunnar remained silent, choosing not to speed their way with one of his tales. Or perhaps, thought Cal, the dwarf's magic was not so powerful in this misty wooded land.

As the light began to fade, and the mists around them

grew darker, they left the forest behind them at last and began hiking across what appeared to be a broad grassy plain. Cal couldn't be sure as the fog still hung heavily, obliterating all but his immediate surroundings. He looked around and noticed that Hathor had stopped and was sniffing at the air.

"Smell death," said the troll.

Gunnar came back to them through the haze. "Yes, Hathor, I don't like the look of this at all. This should be the land of the Skrisung. Yet I do not see or hear any of them about."

They walked on slowly, following the trail, which was now rutted with the tracks of wheeled carts. On their left appeared a silent, deserted house. And another on their right. They passed a broken picket fence and found themselves standing in the middle of a deserted village. There was no wind, no dogs barked, no children squealed. The place was bleak and empty.

"Gives me the creeps!" said Cal, fingering the hilt of his sword. "I wonder where they could all be?"

"Dead," said the troll in a hushed voice. "Smell death everywhere."

Gunnar shook his head sadly and led them on. They passed through the empty street and its ghostly houses and at last left them behind in the gloom. They climbed a low rise, and out of the mists before them loomed the shadowy form of a great wooden hall. As they walked closer, they could see that it had a steep pointed roof and grotesque carvings protruding from the corners. A huge wooden door on the side of the building beckoned to them and Cal started for it.

"Wait," cried the dwarf, grabbing the boy by the sleeve, "'tis death! Stay away from there." Greybeard lead them around the building and back down the gentle slope to a woodpile beneath some trees. It was nearly dark and they were tired.

"Let's build a fire, and camp here for the night." The dwarf opened up his food bag. "Tomorrow will be time enough to solve the mystery of this eerie place."

CHAPTER
12

Caltus Talienson awoke with a start in the middle of the night, threw off his blanket and looked around him. The air was thick with fog, the fire nearly out, and pennons of smoke rose slowly from the faintly glowing coals. He was certain he had heard something, for a chill went up his spine and his hair stood on end. There was an evil presence out in the darkness that he could feel but not see. Next to him, Hathor sat up abruptly and stared intently in the direction of the great hall.

"D'you feel it too?" whispered Cal.

The troll grunted acknowledgment.

"What do you think it is?"

"Don't know," came the hushed reply. "Have bad dream. Hathor in hall on hill. Nasty thing in hall see Hathor!"

"Shh!" Greybeard crept between them, putting his small hands on their shoulders, and spoke softly. "I don't like this one whit. Make no sound, and no matter what you hear, keep still."

The three fell silent, and Cal thought he could make out

a dim yellow glow coming from the direction of the hall. Moments later, a deep, unintelligible voice drifted through the murk to their ears. There was more silence and Cal could hear the pounding of his heart. A bloodcurdling scream pierced the quiet night and then dwindled to the gurgle of a death rattle. Hathor grabbed his axe and stood up, but Greybeard held the troll back. The faint yellow glow went out.

After a long pause with no further action, Hathor dropped his axe, walked over to the woodpile and gathered an arm-load of logs, which he threw onto the fire. Once the coals grew back to a crackling blaze, Cal felt a little safer and he curled up in his blankets. The companions heard no more sounds during the night, but none of them slept very well, if at all.

With the coming of day, the mist thinned and Hathor could see all the way back up the hill to the great hall. He had not slept since the incident during the night yet the troll was certain that someone or something had slipped past his watchful eyes and ears, something that left an evil, malo-dorous scent behind.

"What's that awful smell?" asked Cal, standing up, half yawning.

"Thing that come in the night," said the troll.

"Something we'd best avoid!" The dwarf hopped in front of them with his pack on his back. "Let's head down the road before breakfast and get away from the stench."

The others agreed. Hathor kicked out the remains of the fire and they set out down two rutted tracks, which wound back and forth across a relatively treeless marshy expanse. The mist, albeit thinner, remained, and the skies were a dreary grey, making the dead brown grass through which they walked seem even more lifeless than it was.

Once across the marsh, the path disappeared into a grove of evergreens. The air was fresh here, and smelled of pine trees. Greybeard stopped at the edge of the wood and they sat down atop a dry, grassy hummock to eat their meal and speculate as to what had transpired the night before. In the end the consensus was that whatever they had felt and smelled was the reason the village of the Skrisung was now dead.

"What now, Gunnar?" asked Cal. "If the Skrisung are all dead, how do we find Sjonbrand? Search all the houses, and the great hall . . . and maybe run into that smelly thing . . . and be killed as well?"

The dwarf pulled at his beard, deep in thought. "Maybe so, maybe not." He stared back in the direction of the village.

"Well, Bith would never forgive us if we got ourselves murdered and failed to rescue her from the tower!" declared the boy, smiling.

The troll chuckled but said nothing, just crunched on a particularly large root.

". . . mmm possibly, yes! That's it." The dwarf jumped up with a gleam in his eyes. "We must go to Glasvellir Hall and inquire there."

"How long is this going to take?" asked Cal. "Time is running out for Bith, you know."

"Not long, my friends, not long. Perhaps a day if I tell you a tale . . . and my brothers there should know something of Sjonbrand."

No one could think of a better course of action, and, as none wanted to return to the dead village, they agreed to follow Greybeard to Glasvellir Hall. Moments later, they were packed up and on the trail that led into the woods. The dwarf led the way, singing as usual, in a strange tongue that the others could not comprehend.

The path took the three companions up and down over several low, tree-covered hills, and a pair of song birds sang to them from the treetops, seemingly in answer to the verses chanted by the dwarf. Soon the trees thinned out and as they topped a gentle rise, Hathor stopped and let out a little whistle. Below them on yet another marshy plain was a broad circle of standing stones, and in the center of the ring of stones rose a mound of earth and rocks.

Cal wasn't sure, the mists still obscured much detail, but it looked as if there was a person sitting on the mound. Hathor and the dwarf broke into a trot and Cal had to run to keep up with them. Greybeard led the others between two upright stones and stopped at the base of the mysterious mound. Up close, it could be seen that the mound was not merely rock and earth. It was also full of human skulls and bones, bits of jewelry, pieces of armor, rusting swords, and battered shields. The top alone was covered in lush green grass and, to one side, a rough stone stair wound upward. In the very center of the top of the mound was a sad-looking man, seated on a carved wooden chair inlaid with gold.

" 'Tis a burial mound of the kings of Northunderland." The dwarf spoke in a whisper and pointed at a skeletal hand protruding from under a clump of grass, still bearing gold rings on its fingers. "These are the remains of past kings and nobles of a brave warrior tribe. I would guess this is the burial mound of the Skrisung."

"And the man up there?" asked Cal in a whisper.

"Their king, perhaps. He sits there to gain wisdom and inspiration from the dead in the earth."

Cal glanced at the man atop the mound. "He looks mournful enough to be the king of that dead place."

Greybeard again took the lead and they made their way up the stone stair. The stairs gave way to a gravel trail and the three advanced to a rock slab, set in the ground before the seated man. The sad fellow wore a thick bearskin around his shoulders, and a gold crown rested on his head. A golden breastplate covered his chest, and gold rings and chains adorned his body. Although he was young, deep lines of worry and sorrow furrowed his brow, and his once dark beard was half-tinged with grey. The man sighed, wiped a tear from his eye, and for the first time took note of the three strangers who stood silently in front of him. Staring above them into space, he spoke:

"On your knees before Hrafdi, Grimnison, Boar Killer, Keeper of the Golden Horn, and now King of the Skrisung!" The voice was flat and spoken without feeling or expression. Cal immediately dropped to his knees and bowed. Hathor and the dwarf did likewise.

Greybeard then began to speak, "Noble King Hrafdi, Boar Killer, ruler of the Skri—"

"I have been king since midnight last night," continued the man, taking no further notice of the newcomers. "And tonight at midnight, there will be no king."

The dwarf looked dubiously at Cal and Hathor while the king rambled on.

"One by one we have gone. First the mighty warriors, then the women and children, each in their turn. Night by horrible night, to this last mournful day. To this last fearful night . . ."

The three travelers backed away from the king and held a hushed conference near the edge of the burial mound.

"I think this guy has lost his mind," Cal remarked as he lowered his pack to the ground. "He doesn't even know we're here."

"I think he has a lot on his mind," answered the dwarf. "We have to jar his senses a little!" The dwarf turned to Hathor and pulled off the troll's hat. "Put down your pack,

Thor, and heft your axe before you—look as big and mean as possible!''

The troll puffed up his chest and frowned, holding his weapon ominously over his head. ''Like this?'' he asked.

''Yes, that's it. Now go back over there, stand before Hrafdi's face and snarl.''

Hathor did just that, and after his second guttural rumble, the king blinked and fell silent. The troll lowered his axe and Greybeard stepped before the king once again.

''Noble King, we are travelers from the south, come to seek advice and counsel from the Skrisung.''

The trance which had held the king was broken and he spoke to the three in a soft voice. Introductions were made around and food was offered. The king refused. When Greybeard asked about the fate of the Skrisung, the king related the whole terrible tale.

Until just a few months ago, the Skrisung had been a proud and successful tribe whose warriors, led by the fierce King Grimni, had sailed abroad bringing back plunder, treasure, goats, sheep, and even wives. So successful had they been that the tribal council decided to erect a great wooden meeting hall, where they all could sit and drink to the greater glory of the gods who had so favored them.

A year they spent building the great hall, and craftsmen were called in from faraway kingdoms to help. When it was finished, there was a great feast and celebration that lasted five days and five nights. But alas, at the end of the fifth night, in their moment of greatest glory, there came the undoing of the Skrisung. At midnight, as the exhausted warriors and their women slept around the great table, the doors burst open and in came a great green monster from the sea, a monster which had thirteen eyes and eleven mouths and twoscore and two arms. The thing seized eleven of their thanes and eleven of their wives, and eleven children and devoured them even as they slept.

The next day, King Grimni and his men awoke to the grisly scene of blood and bones, and the trail of death that lead back to the sea. They vowed revenge and the next night set a trap in the great hall, pretending to sleep when came the hour of midnight. The creature came again, and before the king or any of his thanes could spring, it had snatched another warrior and swallowed him whole. The beast then escaped their pursuit down to the sea and vanished beneath the waves.

Each night that followed, the Skrisung lay waiting to do battle with the creature, yet all their tricks and traps failed. The beast avoided a huge pit dug in its path, and refused a pig laced with poison dressed as a warrior and left in the hall. Worst of all, each night another member of the tribe was claimed, until all were gone, thanes, women, and children. .

Hrafdi stood up from his throne, drew a bejewelled sword from his belt and pointed it toward the dead village and its accursed hall. "Yesterday there were but two of us left. Grimni, the king, and myself. Today, I am king. Tonight, I will go to the hall, face the monster, and perchance, slay him. Tomorrow, the Skrisung will be no more. . . ."

A gentle breeze gusted across the mound and at the same time the clouds parted. For a precious moment the scene was bathed in radiant golden sunlight. The glow quickly faded as clouds passed before the sun and Hrafdi slumped back into his throne, dropping his fine sword point-first into the grass underfoot.

CHAPTER
13

Morning had barely come when Bith was wakened by a pounding on the door and an imperious voice demanding that she rise and present herself immediately. Her mind still fogged with sleep and the curious events of the night, she dragged herself to her feet and limped to the door, noting the stiffness in her limbs and the throbbing in her head, no doubt the result of her abrupt meeting with Schlein's door.

Hand to her brow, she stood before the door, composing herself as it swung open, once again revealing the pompous little man still holding the glowing amulet before him and the three muscular guards.

"You are to come with us," the little man said loudly, making certain that the amulet remained between them. "Your lowly presence is once more requested by the Exalted Master." His lip curled as he spoke, and he looked at her with sly, knowing eyes.

Oddly enough, Elizebith did not find herself filled with the usual sense of outrage. Instead, she was strangely calm, almost indifferent to the amulet wielder's insolence and the unwelcome summons. Her composure seemed to annoy the messenger and he began to bait her, like dogs at a fox.

"Schlein has something special planned for you this time," he sneered. "You won't get off so light today!"

But Bith would not be drawn by the man's words, no matter what he said, and she ascended the staircase wrapped in regal dignity.

By the time they reached the carved and painted doorway, Tellarko's face was nearly as red as his striped robes, and Bith was even more firmly in possession of her emotions. No matter what Schlein had planned for her, she was determined not to give in, even if it meant her life. She was uncertain where the great calm had come from. Hers was not normally a peaceful nature, given more to wild, passionate emotions, but seeing the effect such control had on the messenger, she found herself almost anxious to use it against his "Exalted Master." They had robbed her of her magic, but failing to respond to their cruel taunts might prove a weapon in itself.

Without waiting for the door to be opened, Elizebith flung it wide herself, strode boldly into the room and faced Schlein as he sat brooding before the fire.

"Well, what is it now, O Great Exalted Master?" she asked, causing Schlein to look up at her in astonishment.

"Is it to be another proposal of marriage, phrased as beautifully as your first offer? Or perhaps something even more horrible, like dining with you daily for the sake of your dazzling dinner conversation."

As Schlein's eyes bulged in disbelief, Elizebith strolled casually around the room, flicking a grape loose from a cluster, toying with a quarter of a chicken and then tossing it to the floor and wiping her fingers daintily upon a napkin as though the meat had been found unworthy of her attentions.

Schlein lifted himself halfway out of his chair, his face

suffused with a dark crimson flood of rage as Bith lifted a crystal flagon of wine and held it up to the light.

"Now listen to me, young lady. I've been very patient with you up to now. . . ."

Bith's nose wrinkled in distaste and she set the flagon down on the edge of the table, where it teetered momentarily and then crashed to the floor, staining the flagstones a dark shade of burgundy. Schlein was dumbfounded, for the wine had been the last of a truly great vintage and not even his considerable powers could replace it. And there was little, other than death, torture and destruction, that Schlein liked more than a good glass of wine.

Elizebith, however, seemed to care not a fig for what she had done. Schlein saw her advance toward a cask of Anselmic Brandy which was brewed from the entire harvest of a single remote mountain valley and distilled over and over again, until the resulting liquor was as thick and heavy and sweet as honey. It took one hundred such harvests to fill a cask such as this one and another hundred years to age it properly. There were no other casks left anywhere on either side of the Mistwall that Schlein knew of and he prized it greatly, allowing himself but a single thimbleful, and that only on very special occasions.

"Wait! Don't touch—!" he said, taking a step forward and holding out a desperate hand.

Elizebith turned toward him as he spoke and somehow, without even seeming to touch it, knocked the cask off its stand, fell to the floor where it bounced once—miraculously without breaking—and then, before Schlein could reach it, rolled straight into the fireplace like a thing possessed. The Exalted Master cried out in horror and flung himself forward in a desperate attempt to rescue the precious cask. But he was too late. A single drop escaping from the edge of the cork ignited and then the entire cask exploded, hurling a solid sheet of flaming alcohol out across the room.

Schlein, positioned as he was between Bith and the fire, received the full force of the wave of flaming spirits. If an observer had been present he would have seen the sheet of fire part as it passed Bith, leaving her unharmed. Schlein was not so fortunate. As it struck him, it adhered to his flesh, where it sizzled and burned, feeding greedily on the layer of grease that coated his vast body. It crackled and bit through the coarse hair that covered his bare chest, and a stink like burning chicken feathers filled the chamber. Schlein staggered back, screaming horribly, beating at his body and clutching his face with his seared hands, knocking over the table and its burden of food, crystal and china and stumbling and falling among the debris.

"Well, did you want something or not?" Elizebith said, as though nothing out of the ordinary had happened, staring down at a groaning Schlein, who lay among the ruins of his feast. "I have better things to do with my time than stand around while you play with your food."

Schlein took his hands down from his ruined face and stared in disbelief at Elizebith. It was difficult to read his expression, for his face had been badly burned and was already beginning to swell. Large blisters filled with a watery fluid began to rise, distorting his face even further. His eyebrows had been burned away, as well as his eyelashes, and his hair reduced to a frizzled crisp. Elizebith studied Schlein dispassionately and decided that his expression contained equal amounts of indelible rage, insufferable pain, and total disbelief.

"Well, if you've nothing better to do than lie there, I guess I'll go back to my room," Bith said lightly and, turning on her heel, swept out of the room, somehow managing to bring down an entire rack of crystal goblets, the only thing of value left standing in the all-but-demolished room.

Bith paced through the open doorway, head tilted at an imperious angle, and swept back down the spiral stair. The three guards and the magician Tellarko peered cautiously into the room and gaped at the destruction within, as well as the incredible sight of their lord and master lying sprawled in the foodstuffs like some great wounded boar. The room was filled with thick, black smoke as the precious hand-woven carpet of many colors, the handcarved ebony furniture and the figured silk tapestries reduced themselves to embers.

The foursome gawked at Schlein with open mouths before they realized that if they could see him, he could most certainly see them, and it seemed most unlikely that he would allow anyone who viewed him in such a state to remain alive to tell the tale to others. Hastily withdrawing, they turned and hurried down the stairs after Bith, who had gone on without them, proceeding at a stately pace until she reached the tower room. She entered the room without even a backward glance and then slammed the door in their astonished faces, leaving them to wring their hands and worry about their own lives.

Eventually, after much whispering, the guards took it upon themselves to vanish completely, daring to hope that Schlein's injuries would serve as a distraction and enable them to flee beyond his reach before he was able to bring his full powers to bear in the search.

Tellarko elected to remain, for he had nowhere else to go and had invested too many years in Schlein's service to abandon it so lightly. He decided to approach his lord with concern and great empathy and offer his services to take revenge upon she who had caused him such great injury. If he could direct Schlein's anger onto the girl, where it rightly belonged, perhaps Schlein would not see fit to place too much of the blame upon him. Perhaps he would only be thrown against a stone wall, or through a closed oaken door.

If that failed to work, Tellarko would offer up the guards whose lives mattered but little to him. Working out his plan, he filled his pouches with unguents and soothing ointments and hurried off to salve his master's wounded pride and body. Only for a moment did he pause to wonder how it was that one little slip of a girl, deprived of her magic, could have brought such great destruction down upon the powerful Schlein.

Meanwhile, back in her room, Bith was sitting on her cushions, wondering the same thing herself. She played the sequence of events over in her head, time and time again, from the first moment she heard the summons to the moment she reentered her room and slammed the door of her own volition.

For the first time the room seemed a safe harbor, a welcome place rather than a prison, and she studied its cold, bare walls and realized for the first time that things could indeed be worse.

She was entrapped and her magic was gone, but she was still alive and where there was life, there was always hope. There was also the fact of her unknown helper, and help her he had. Had he not brought her food and drink and blankets and cushions, her state would be far more desperate and she might not have had the strength or the courage to resist Schlein's demands. Once again she wondered as to her mysterious helper's identity and his purpose in aiding her. But such a thing was not to be known and for the moment it was enough that there was help to be had.

Elizebith looked down and saw the two round amber balls

which she held in her hand and became aware that she had
been holding them for some time. She could not remember
picking them up, yet she could not remember being without
them since they had been given to her by her mysterious
friend. They had been with her during her ascent to Schlein's
chambers and throughout the entire episode.

She stared at the stones curiously, bringing them closer
so that she might study them. They appeared to be but simple
stones at first glance, but close examination revealed them
to be far more. They were a deep, clear, rich shade of amber
that invited one's gaze, drawing the eye deeper and deeper
into their crystalline depths. Tiny objects were contained in
the heart of the stones. Here was a tiny, perfect leaf, rich
green in the center but tinged with red along the edges. And
there, there was a miniscule beetle, midnight black in color,
its carapace an iridescent rainbow of rose and teal and pur-
ple. And here was a tiny, tiny snail, with a tall, winding
cone of pinkish shell, frozen in mid-crawl upon a bit of
twig for all of eternity.

Bith stared into the depths of the stones, and as she studied
them she felt a great calm descend upon her troubled mind.
Strength flowed into her and she nodded once, as though
to herself, knowing that when next she faced Schlein, she
would take with her the strength gained from this encounter.

Deep in the dungeon of that same tower, Endril was
having difficulties with his own resolve. Carving out the
wood behind the hinges of the door was proving harder than
he had anticipated. At first the going had been easy, for the
wood had absorbed the moisture of the dungeon for centuries
and had all but crumbled under their assault. But the door
was made of oak, and while the outer layers might have
fallen prey to the passage of the years, the heart of the solid
slab had remained firm. If anything, it had grown harder,

more dense with age, and as they progressed it was the file which gave way rather than the wood.

Endril and Purkins stared at the bent file with dismay, for it had been straightened and reshaped too many times. The metal itself was stressed and beginning to break. It seemed as though their plan had come to a dismal halt.

The two of them sat side by side in the darkness, listening to the familiar clatter of the knucklebones in the guards' room beyond and the even more familiar cursing as the orcan guards accused one another of cheating.

The conversations were easily overheard, for their door was immediately adjacent to the guards' chambers. There was little to hear, save the rattle of knucklebones and complaints about their dismal lives, which seemed only a cut above those whom they were set to guard. Endril often found himself thinking that they were just as much prisoners as those caged within the cells.

The guards' rations were surely larger, and they received a generous tot of grog each night, and once a month they were allowed a day of leisure, but there were few other benefits. The orcs were always complaining about their wages: four coppers a month, with room and board deducted from that unprincely sum as a further insult.

The knucklebones and eating provided their sole form of entertainment, and even this was a questionable enjoyment, for their level of intelligence was not very great and they were all but unable to wager cleverly or conceal their limited strategies from each other. Also, having been forced into each other's company for so long, even their dim brains had figured out what each of them was likely to do in a particular circumstance. Under these conditions, it was not surprising that there were few big winners and the same few coppers circulated among them, first in this pocket and then in that one, never residing there long enough to buy its owner anything of value, had there been anything of value for them to buy.

The single exception to this unhappy circle was an unfortunate orc by the name of Bebo. Bebo was larger and even more stupid than his companions and was also saddled with a stammer and a stutter that grew more severe when he was unhappy. Which was all the time. Bebo served as the cruel butt for all his companions' hostilities, resentments, and miseries. Bebo-baiting was a time-honored tradition in the dungeon.

Even Endril found himself feeling sorry for the unfortunate orc, and he began to wonder if the creature might not in some way be used to bring about an escape. He even dreamed about it, but so far, no such plan had presented itself and that, coupled with the destruction of their single digging implement, plunged Endril into the deepest of despairs.

"Hey, what are you guys doin'?" asked a tiny voice, causing Endril and Purkins to leap to their feet and look about them wildly, searching for the unseen speaker.

"I mean, you wuz doin' pretty good there for a while, but now you've given up. How does you intends to get outta here that way, sittin' there starin' at 'cher toes?"

The elf was not sure whether he heard the voice, or if it was a trick in his mind, not unlike the voice of Vili, heard so long ago in his sleep. "Who, who is that?" asked Endril. "Did you hear anything, John Purkins? Who's talking? Show yourself!"

"It's me!" said a dark shape which detached itself from the deeper darkness of the corner and stood under the tiny trickle of light which entered the cell from the outer chamber.

"Why, it's a . . . rat!" Purkins said, casting about for something to throw at the foul creature.

"No, wait . . . I think it is the same creature who brought me the note from my friends," said Endril. "Do not harm him." The elf held out an arm, and the shadowy black figure hopped on to his sleeve. "Greetings, Master Rat, you are welcome in our cell. What are you called?"

"Well, I am See-In-The-Dark of Shadowvale Cave, but most folks just call me Blackwhiskers."

"You are aptly named, Master Rat. But tell me, have you always gone about speaking to men and elves?"

The rat puzzled for a moment and then answered, "To tell the truth, no. I never even spoke to a big one before that old geezer called me, uh, old—what's his name, uh . . ."

"Not Gunnar Greybeard?"

"That's the very same guy I was mentionin'! He sang this weird song, ya know, and then tole. me all this special stuff. I'm a real lucky rat! He coulda picked someone else!"

"I'd say we're the lucky ones," said Endril, smiling. "To what do we owe the honor of your visit?"

"Oh, well, uh, I was just wonderin' how you guys were doin', you know, how you was makin' out. Thought I'd come back an' check on you. Also, the grub's pretty tasty here. Much better than the cave where I come from. An' it's excitin' here, ya know? There's all kinds a neat stuff that I never seen before. An' all my cousins, well, I never met none of 'em before and they're a pretty good bunch a guys. They sure know how to throw a great party. There's always good stuff lyin' around here, just waitin' to be picked up. Fer instance, yesterday, the head guy who owns this joint had some kind of fight with a lady and she wrecked the place. There was food everywhere. Boy, we sure ate good last night. An then I thought, wonder how those guys are doin' . . . maybe I'll go see. But 'cher just sittin' here not doin' nothin'. So what gives?"

"A lady?" asked Endril, trying to follow the rat's somewhat rambling train of thought and pick out the meaning.

"Yeah, some girl the head guy keeps locked up in the tower. They had a big fight and she almost wrecked the place, you shoulda seen it, food everywhere an'—"

"Wait, Blackwhiskers. Speak more slowly, I beg of you," said Endril. "This lady, can you describe her to me?"

"Describe her? Hmmm, I don't know, all you human types look alike to me but, well, her fur is long and black-like, and her eyes are a real creepy silver color, an' her ears are way too small to hear anything and her nose can't even wiggle! She's real ordinary, looks just like all of you guys. Nuthin' special."

"Did you catch her name?" asked Endril, his heart pounding in his chest, for he thought that he recognized Bith in the rat's description. Bith was still here in the tower! It was almost too much to be believed! But what did this Murcroft have in mind?

Blackwhiskers shook his head.

"Tell me, Master Rat," Endril said softly, "this fight. What was it about? Was the girl all right?"

"Oh, yeah, she did a real number on this guy, wrecked the place good. Cooked his face for him an' burned him all over, he was real mad! I saw the whole thing myself! Nothin' like that ever happens at home!"

So Murcroft and Bith had had an encounter and Bith had won. . . . For the moment Endril mused upon the odd turn of events, wondering what was going on and how he could tell Bith of his whereabouts and maybe . . . and then an idea struck him!

"Master Rat, your kind interest in our affairs has been much appreciated," Endril said warmly. "Unfortunately, my friends and I are not in a position to repay your kindness at this moment, but if you would allow yourself to become further involved with our petty affairs, our gratitude would be even greater and at some point in the future . . ."

"Say no more!" cried the rat as he leaped upon Endril's knee and waved his little paws in the air. "I'm yers! This is more fun than a barrel o' voles! What'cha want me ta do?"

And, drawing the rat close, Endril began to speak.

CHAPTER
14

Cal jumped forward and grabbed King Hrafdi's sword from where it was stuck in the sod at their feet. Lovingly, he pulled it free and wiped the tip of the blade against his pants leg to remove the dirt. The boy then produced a small cloth and buffed the blade to a shine. He held the sword up to the sky, squinted down the edge and then offered it to its owner.

"Sire," pleaded the boy, "there are three of us, and we are not without fighting skills. Is there some way we can help you to slay this monster?"

Hrafdi brushed a tear from his cheek, leaned forward and reclaimed his sword, carefully resheathing it at his belt. "No, I fear not, young man. This is my peril, not yours. The curse of the Skrisung weighs heavily on my shoulders. It is my doom, and my doom alone. And alone against it I must stand or die."

There was a brief silence and Greybeard edged up beside Cal to speak: "Ahem! Noble King, we are here in your lands," said the dwarf with a bow and a flourish, "to seek the sword Sjonbrand, known as the Skryling's blade. Per-

133

haps Your Majesty has heard tell of this great weapon.''

Hrafdi nodded silently.

''We have come a thousand leagues in our quest!''

''And if we find it,'' added Cal, ''could I not use it to slay this creature with thirteen eyes, eleven mouths, and twoscore and two arms!''

The king shifted uncomfortably in his golden chair. ''No, such a thing is beyond hope. It has already been tried. Sjonbrand may not be wielded by the Skrisung. King Grimni thought as much and went to great lengths to bring it hither, for surely a sword blessed with such great powers would save us from our curse. He and four thanes went forth to gain the sword, yet the king returned alone with the great weapon, after much pain and tribulation. What's more, at the moment of truth, this thing gained at such expense, Sjonbrand, would not come out of its sheath. It refused to serve and my lord stood helpless and we watched in horror as the monster carried off his queen.''

The dwarf jumped up and down with excitement. ''It's here? You have Sjonbrand here, now?''

Cal's pulse quickened, and Hathor grinned at the boy, slapping him on the shoulder.

''Nay,'' came the sad reply, ''it stayed not among the Skrisung. The next day in anger, Grimni cast the sword down the well in the center of the village.''

''Then we shall seek it there!'' exclaimed the dwarf triumphantly.

''Nay,'' said the king again, ''you shall not find Sjonbrand there, for it was taken during the night by the Finngalkin, who carried it off to her lair. She will not part with such a treasure lightly.''

''The Finngalkin?'' asked Hathor.

The king continued, unheeding, ''Besides, since the sword may not be wielded by the Skrisung, it can be of no

possible use to . . ." A sudden realization came to the king
and his eyes lit up with excitement.

"We are not of the Skrisung," said Cal slowly, smiling.
He tapped himself on the chest with his fist. "I am a fighter,
come over the sea from afar! I can use Sjonbrand. I *will*
use Sjonbrand . . . and with it I will slay your monster."

The king looked into Cal's eyes. "By the gods, you just
may be able—"

"Tell us where we may find this Finngalkin," interrupted
the dwarf excitedly.

"And what do we need to do when we meet her," added
the boy.

"What is Finngalkin?" the troll asked again.

Hrafdi was nearly oblivious to the barrage of questions
and rubbed his hand across his brow for a moment.

"The Finngalkin . . ." The king stood up again in a daze
and pointed vaguely off to the West. "Go quickly through
the wood and beyond the hill to the clearing where dwells
the she-creature, the Finngalkin. She has possession of the
sword, Sjonbrand. You must persuade her to give it up . . .
your cause is just."

"Is she dangerous? Do we slay her?" asked Cal.

"When you meet her, you must let your heart be your
guide. Make haste now, midnight tonight comes my time
to guard the meeting hall of the Skrisung."

"But—"

The dwarf tugged at Cal's sleeve. "Time's a'wasting!
We know what we need to know. Let's be off."

Hathor shook his head disgustedly.

Greybeard led the others down off the mound, through
the ring of stones and out across the marsh. The going was
a bit difficult at first as their feet, at least Cal's and Hathor's,
kept sinking into the slushy mire between the clumps of
grass. At last the ground began to rise and the terrain became

drier and the three rapidly approached the wood on the western side of the marsh.

They came to the edge of the forest and the dwarf headed north, searching for a path or trail.

"There should be one here somewhere," he remarked, almost to himself. They stumbled along through the grass until Greybeard turned abruptly and pointed to a worn place that exited a thick grove of trees and led back across the marsh. "Here we go!"

Cal turned back and glanced one last time at the distant king Hrafdi, still seated on his throne on top of the burial mound. The boy waved, and, a moment later the king stood and waved back. The three then plunged forward into the dense growth of trees. It was a narrow path and the branches hung low, sometimes across their way, and Hathor complained each time Cal slapped him in the face with a pine bough.

The trail took them to the top of a ridge and followed the curves of the hill for a time. The trees were thinner here and in the breaks Cal thought he could make out a broad, treeless valley through the mists in the distance. Was this the hill beyond which lay the Finngalkin?

"What is Finngalkin?" asked the troll one last time.

"Well," began the dwarf, "all I know—" They had just started down the far slope when Greybeard stopped. There before the three companions stood Lennia and the trio of female trolls they had so recently left behind in the forest of Auseviget.

"We meet again, Gunnar Greybeard," the troll queen said in a deep, sultry voice. She cast a longing glance at Hathor, fluttering her lashes at him. Her chest heaved invitingly and Hathor could not take his eyes off her perfect troll body.

"No time to stop and chat, foster mother," the dwarf

said nervously. "I thank you for the advice you gave us about Sjonbrand. The great sword has been found and we are this close to our goal!" He held two fingers together above him in the air.

"We have attained our goal as well," murmured the queen, extending her hand to Hathor, who graciously took it in his huge paw. She led the glassy-eyed troll to the side of the path. "We have come to collect on a promise made."

"No, you can't . . ."

"Silence, Gunnar!" Lennia flashed her troll fangs menacingly at the dwarf. "The future of trollkind in Northunderland is at stake, and we will not be denied. Tonight, under the great hill of Auseviget there will be a troll assembly. Your friend can be of no help where you are going. Our need for Hathor is greater than yours. Tonight he belongs to the troll women."

"But . . . but . . ." stuttered Cal.

The other troll women gathered around Hathor, putting their arms around his great shoulders, and whispered into his ears, giggling.

Cal grabbed Greybeard's shoulder. "Do something! Sing a song! Tell a tale! Stop them!"

Hathor was led off like a sheep into the forest by Lennia and the troll women while the boy and the dwarf stood together on the trail staring after them in stunned disbelief.

Gunnar shook his head glumly. "Sorry. That was a request we could not refuse. I guess we'll just have to make do without his help. I'm certain you can handle the task ahead." He slapped the boy on the back. "But don't worry about Hathor. Unless I miss my guess he'll be having the time of his life tonight."

"Yeah, sure. While we have to face the Finngalkin, whatever that is, and then slay that awful monster with thousands of eyes and arms and things, Thor is out romping in the woods with a herd of naked troll women!''

''You'd rather be in his shoes? That is, if he wore any shoes.''

The boy nodded, thinking of the chunky bodies that had just disappeared into the wood. ''I'll say!''

''Well you aren't! So what do you intend to do? Stand here till midnight?'' asked the dwarf, tugging at the boy's sleeve. ''The Finngalkin and Sjonbrand await our pleasure.''

Reluctantly, Cal turned and smiled at his lone companion, and the four-plus-one-minus-three started once again down the narrow trail through the forest.

''Just what is a Finngalkin anyway?'' asked Cal as he rounded a bend, walked past Greybeard, and ducked under a low-hanging branch. The dwarf had stopped and was gathering some rocks from the side of the trail. He filled a pouch and then hurried after the boy.

''Well, to tell the truth, I've never seen one, and old Gevrym, my teacher, mentioned one only once in the tale of the Miller's daughter and the Golden Egg . . . or was it the Story of the Walking Tree of Evenau? Or was that the sorcerer who turned himself into a chicken? But who knows about a story? In any case, they can be very tricky.''

''Especially your tall tales, Gunnar,'' laughed Cal. ''But you, too, can be very tricky at times. That's no help to me. You must know more than that. Tell me now, what did your teacher say about the Finngalkin?''

Greybeard did not reply. Cal shrugged, and plodded along the path. He came to a place where two trees crossed overhead, ducked under another branch and stopped. When he turned to say, ''I'm thirsty. How about a drink of that wine?'' Greybeard was nowhere to be seen. Cal whirled around anxiously, looking in all directions, but the dwarf was gone. Cal ran back up the trail, crying aloud.

"Greybeard! Where are you?"

He stopped when he came to the place where they had lost Hathor and turned back disgustedly. He searched on either side of the trail again and then kicked his foot in the dirt. Something on the ground caught his eye. There were some stones arranged in a pattern on the path. The boy circled around and kneeled down to study them. The stones spelled out the word *tricky*.

"This is a fine mess," Cal grumbled to himself. He wondered for a moment if this was all some sort of evil plan devised by Schlein to separate the four. If it were, it had surely succeeded. "Dammit anyhow!" he cursed.

Greybeard's voice came out of nowhere:

"Mina rvoksi, have no fear.
Kule, paiva, Sjonbrand is near."

Then, as an afterthought, the voice of the unseen dwarf continued, "Now, off with you . . . finish the quest! I'll meet you at the beach. You know the way."

The boy took a deep breath. "No one to help me now. Caltus Talienson, you're on your own!"

His thoughts turned once again to Bith and he resolved to go on alone despite the desertion of his companions. So it was that the four-plus-one-minus-four set out to face the Finngalkin of Northunderland, whatever that might be.

CHAPTER
15

Now that he was alone, Cal became more aware of the sounds, or rather, the lack of sounds in the forest that surrounded him. As he stalked warily among the trees, he decided to draw his sword . . . to be ready just in case. After half an hour of this his wrist grew tired.

"Just in case, of what?" he muttered to himself. He had not seen or heard anything besides an extremely small ground squirrel that skittered across the forest floor at his noisy approach. Cal shoved his sword back into its sheath and massaged his sore arm. He tried whistling the few tunes that he knew. That seemed to work, for he made better progress now that he was unable to hear the slightest snap of a twig or rustle of a branch in the wind.

He was still thirsty, of course, and cursed the dwarf again for deserting him before he'd gotten a drink from the wine bottle. Cal was quite pleased when at last he came to a broad, roaring stream that rushed down from the mountains, now visible on his left. The mist was fading fast, and the sun was about to make its first real appearance since he had arrived in Northunderland. The boy dropped his pack and lay in the grass leaning over the mossy bank. He splashed cold water on his face and in his hair and then drank his fill. If he wasn't in such a hurry, he would have taken time for a cold bath. The water was crystal clear and ever so inviting.

As he rose, refreshed, and shouldered his pack, he noticed for the first time that there seemed to be a rude hut of some sort at the far side of a clearing on the other side of the stream. Could this be it? His pulse quickened, and he searched for a way to cross. There were no stepping stones to be seen in either direction, so there was nothing to do but plunge into the water and wade across. At its deepest point the stream came up to his knees.

Cal climbed out of the water and shook out his boots. He really ought to wring out his pants out . . . but no, he glanced across the clearing again. It was definitely a shack, a small wooden shack thrown together out of sticks, branches, and a few logs. A wisp of blue smoke curled up through a hole, actually several holes, in the roof. He walked slowly forward, his boots squishing as he went, all thought of fear gone from his mind. Sjonbrand was here. He could feel it!

The boy had walked halfway across the clearing when the door, or possibly a wall of the little hut began to shake vigorously. He heard some cursing, and then the whole side of the shack shuddered and tumbled to the ground with a sudden loud crash.

"Whoof! Gonna have to get that fixed!" said a pleasant female voice from within. Then, to Cal's amazement, out through the side of the shack came just about the ugliest, well, strangest creature he had ever seen. The thing stumbled over the fallen side of its shack and tumbled to the ground in a heap.

"Ooops! Sorry. Not at my best today." The Finngalkin

struggled to its feet in front of a dumbstruck Caltus Talienson. It had the upper torso of a large woman, and the head
and hind quarters of a horse. She stood up unsteadily on
her hooves, swishing her long black tail from side to side.
Cal's eyes opened wide. She was holding the sword, Sjonbrand, in her arms.

"Hi there, sweetie! Oh, my, you are a cute one aren't
you? Let's see if old Gertie can guess why you've come."
She shook her head and her mane flapped pleasantly to either
side. Cal thought he heard her whinny as well.

"A . . . are you the Finngalkin?" he asked timidly.

"That I am, dearie, the only one in Northunderland. Freyr
and Freya! For all I know, I may be the only one in the
whole world, for never have I met another such as myself!"
She laughed cheerfully and stepped a little closer to the boy.
"Now, would this be what you have come for, my dear?"
Just as the sun broke through the clouds she held the sword
up, tantalizing her visitor.

Cal's heart skipped a beat. That was it! Sjonbrand! The
weapon called out to him, begging the boy to take it in his
hand. He stood transfixed by its beauty. The runes along
the blade danced in his head, and the jewels in the hilt
sparkled brilliantly in the sunlight. The blade caught the sun
and the flash temporarily blinded him.

"Yes! Yes!" he cried out passionately.

"Well, no problem, sweetheart. It can easily be yours,
but of course you'll have to do old Gertie a little favor."
She turned her head to one side and looked at him with her
big soft brown eyes.

"Name it!" said Cal resolutely.

The Finngalkin smiled and a mouthful of shiny white
teeth twinkled in the sunlight.

"Give us a big hug and a kiss!" So saying, she tossed

the sword up into the sky and held her arms out to the boy, expectantly, invitingly.

Cal swallowed hard. *Phew*, she was ugly . . . yet she seemed somehow sweet, and beauty was not always . . . Hrafdi had said to follow your heart. His heart melted and the boy rushed forward, sweeping the she-creature into his arms, and planted a kiss square on her enormous lips.

Sjonbrand fell to the ground with a thump, point first, right where he had been standing just a moment before. Cal saw the sword out of the corner of his eye, and the hairs on the back of his neck stood on end.

"You are a wise young man!" exclaimed the Finngalkin into his ear with a giggle. "The sword is yours . . . but first, dearie, let's have another kiss!" She grabbed Cal more tightly and bent him over backward, planting her gaping maw over his face, nearly sucking the breath out of his lungs.

"Phew!" the boy gasped breathlessly when the Finngalkin released her iron grip on his body. "You're one hell of a kisser!"

"Why, thank you, sweetie, you're not bad yourself." She brushed her mane back to one side and swished her tail invitingly. "How's about sticking around for a while and keeping me company? It gets pretty lonely for an old girl like me up here in the woods at night. A strong young man could change my life!"

Cal stroked her gently. "Nothing would please me more . . . Gertie? Is that your name?"

The she-creature nodded.

"But the lives of others hang in the balance. It's not that I don't want to stay. But if I—"

"Don't tell me," interrupted the Finngalkin, "I know the story. If you don't rescue the fair maiden who's locked up in the tower . . . Believe you me, nobody ever comes to me for a magic sword just to hang it on his wall! But that's all right, I understand.'' She grabbed him by the shoulders. "By the way, what's your name, darling?''

"Caltus Talienson.''

"A fine warrior name.'' She walked in a circle around him, eyeing him carefully. "Now, before you go off to your dirty old battle, let old Gertie do you a favor. A special favor, because I like you.'' The Finngalkin nudged him with her hip. "Who knows, maybe some day you'll come back and stay with me for a spell. That would be charming. We'll soon find out what's in store for you.''

She tugged at his pack, pulling it from his shoulders, and tossed it to the ground. Then she opened his shirt and took it off. Gertie bade him sit in the grass and she yanked off both his wet boots and then pulled down his trousers. Soon he stood naked before her.

"What . . .''

"Shh, trust me, sweetie. Not every man who comes this way gets the treatment. This won't take but a minute.'' The strange horse-woman closed her eyes and began to chant to herself. She ran her hands slowly, gently, over his body, leaving no place untouched.

A few moments later she opened her eyes and put her soft hands to his cheeks and looked him in the eyes. "You will receive no wounds!'' she declared confidently. "Go forth to battle. You may slay your monsters without fear, for no harm is on your body!''

Cal frowned, not fully understanding what had just taken place.

"What's this gloom, Caltus, let's have a smile! Old Gertie can see into the future. You've just passed the test of the warrior.'' She slapped him playfully on his bare behind. He broke into a grin and thanked her.

Cal made a small fire, and while he dried out his boots,

the Finngalkin cooked a steaming pot of oatmeal, which she insisted on sharing before she would let her young companion depart. Soon he was dressed and the two of them pushed the wall of her hut back into place. At last Cal was ready to go, and as he reached to pull Sjonbrand from the ground Gertie grabbed his wrist.

"Use it only for good, and no harm will ever come to you as long as Sjonbrand is at your side."

He leaned forward and kissed her on the cheek one last time and then grasped the sword. His hand tingled with energy the moment he touched the hilt, and the life-force in the blade surged into his body. Cal became light-headed, yet his thoughts were now clearer than ever. Hope and courage welled in his breast. He had become invincible! He had felt this way once before in his life. Once before when he had wielded the Runesword of Vili at Cairngorm. So! This too was a Runesword! Had Vili tricked him? The boy laughed out loud. At the moment he really didn't care.

Cal's old sword, a prize from the battle at Cairngorm, jumped out of its sheath and landed with a clatter on the gravel beside him. Gertie scooped it up and held it to her breast. She grinned at the boy.

"I'll just keep this as a token of your esteem! If you ever need it again, you know where to find it. Now off with you! You have lives to save!"

Sjonbrand slid effortlessly into his sheath. Cal threw his boots and his pack over his shoulder and trotted over to the stream. He stopped and looked back one last time before wading across.

"Thanks, Gertie!"

The Finngalkin blew him an oversized kiss that literally knocked him into the water.

•   •   •

Hathor followed the women, not knowing or caring where they were taking him. He was in a daze. The smell of them drove him wild, their touch made him tingle, and when they whispered in his ears, he shivered with pleasure. Feelings were aroused that he never knew existed.

As he floated dream-like through the sweet-smelling forest, Hathor let his hands wander where they would, eagerly seeking out and touching the mounds of soft troll flesh that surrounded him. His loins ached and he could not hide his arousal. The troll women laughed, and pulled off his human garments.

They took him at last to a wide, green, sunlit vale. No ordinary valley this, for it was filled with a sight that would be forever etched on Hathor's mind, a sight that would bring a smile to his lips to his dying day; for the place was alive, as far as his eyes could see, with voluptuous, naked troll women, all hungry for the one troll man in all of Northunderland.

Hathor was led through the man-hungry throng of troll women to a small rise at one side of the valley, where a gaily decorated tent had been erected. There, speeches were given which the numbed Hathor did not quite hear . . . something about the order of precedence and the restoration of former glory . . . he couldn't be sure, for speeches were the last thing on his mind. They made him stand, and a great cheer rang out. Then Lennia came to him and Hathor was quickly and pleasantly pinned to the ground by the press of a thousand soft, warm bodies.

CHAPTER
16

The return through the forest to the burial mound went by in a flash. As Cal moved speedily along the twisting path, ducking branches, leaping stones, it felt to him as though Greybeard were spinning another of his travel tales. When he reached the edge of the marsh he could see Hrafdi, still seated in the distance. The sun had by now sunk below the horizon and the few clouds left in the sky glowed pink, casting a pleasant rosy glow over the scene.

"Haloo!" Cal hailed. The king jumped to his feet and called out excitedly. The boy broke into a run and trotted across the marshy ground effortlessly, not once sinking into the mire.

"Congratulations, Caltus Talienson," proclaimed Hrafdi as the boy stood before the king. "I see you have met and tamed the Finngalkin and that Sjonbrand is yours." Hrafdi, now all smiles, winked at Cal. "Pray tell me, young man, how did you manage to get around the she-creature's tricks?"

Cal told the story of the ramshackle hut, and the Finngalkin's disturbing countenance, and the fateful invitation to kiss and hug the creature. Then he told of the sword which she threw high into the air and how it fell to earth where he had stood but a moment before.

"Well done. Well done. A lesser man would have hesitated too long, she would have had a meal, and I would still be doomed to my dire fate. Perchance, Sjonbrand has come at last to serve the Skrisung in their final hour." The king stood up and put his hand on Cal's shoulder. "Just to allay my last fears, Caltus, would you be so kind as to draw Sjonbrand from the sheath. Prove to me that you, indeed, may wield it in battle."

The boy stepped back, grasped the hilt, and the sword literally jumped out of the scabbard with a metallic ring. It had a life of its own and flew through the air in swipes and circles as though Cal were fighting an invisible opponent. The boy, thoroughly caught up in the activities of the willful sword, paced forward and back, lunging with his body, sidestepping, and executing dazzling pirouettes as though in a ballet.

Hrafdi cheered and began to clap, but stopped abruptly when he had to duck for his life as the tip of the sword whizzed dangerously close to his head. The boy and the Runesword circled the throne twice until, at last, the display came to an end, and Cal slipped the fantastic blade back into its sheath.

"Sjonbrand and I are one, Your Majesty!" the boy said proudly.

"So I see. And I should be green with envy. Would that I had such a sword in my belt." He drew his own fine weapon and ran his fingers along the edge of the blade. "Yet Hrafnir, as my weapon is called, has served me long and well, for here I still stand, living testament to its power, alive and alone among the Skrisung."

He slid his sword back into his belt, turned to Cal and

sighed. "Would that my people still lived to see your coming . . . or that you had come but a month ago." Hrafdi put his arm around Cal's shoulder. "But what's done is done. Come, follow me to my house. We must prepare for our meeting tonight with the beast in the hall."

The two climbed down from the mound, and walked in the twilight through the standing stones, the king leading the way easily through the small wood and back across the marsh toward the deserted village. He stopped and shook his head sadly as the great hall, with its grotesque carvings, loomed above them.

"We built that hall to celebrate our fame, fortune, and success, but alas, since it was finished it has been our ruin. Surely we have offended one of the gods to bring such an awful curse down upon us. No sacrifice we made would stop the beast. Deserted by our gods, we were." He looked at Cal and tapped Sjonbrand on the hilt. "Yet someone has come to my rescue at last."

Hrafdi gave the grim hall a wide berth and circled around it to the village which lay silent in the darkness. They passed several small houses and came to a path paved with crushed rock which led to a large wooden building with a steep pointed roof. The king pushed open a low door that squeaked noisily, and walked in.

"Welcome to my humble abode," Hrafdi said from within. There was a smack of flint, and the king reappeared with a lit torch. "Please come in."

Cal ducked through the entrance and followed Hrafdi through a long, narrow room. The dirt floor was covered with broken crockery, wooden spoons, and an occasional overturned bench or chair. His host pulled a dusty curtain aside and entered a larger chamber at the far end. He quickly lit two more torches set in the walls, which gave the place a warm if feeble illumination. The whole house was covered with dust inside, and smacked of disuse. Hrafdi slumped down in a chair at one end of a rough-hewn table and hefted a fat crockery bottle to his lips. After a long draught, he invited Cal to join him.

"To fortify our spirits ere we face the foe!"

Cal took a swig from the jug and immediately wished he hadn't. The liquor attacked his throat and burned all the way down. He shook his head.

"Wuff!" exclaimed the boy, his eyes watering. "What was that stuff?"

The king smiled at him. "Quite a bite to it, eh? That's from the last batch of mead we brewed before the monster fell upon us. I fear it has gotten a bit stronger with age. Be patient, it grows smoother with each swallow!"

"I can believe that!" Cal was already feeling a bit woozy. "But I think I've had enough for now. Shouldn't we be getting over to the great hall? What if the monster arrives early?"

Hrafdi slammed the jug down on the table. "First we need a plan. Then we set the trap." He got up and walked over to an iron-bound wooden chest that was wedged up against the wall. After rummaging around for a while, he held up a dented spiral horn.

"Behold the horn of the Skrisung!"

When it was placed before him, Cal could see that the instrument was made of solid gold. The boy picked it up and put it to his lips.

"Nay, nay!" yelped Hrafdi, "do not sound the horn now, 'twill bring down my house! I shall blow it tonight, just before we face the beast with thirteen eyes, eleven mouths, and twoscore and two arms." Hrafdi bent down over the table and glanced from side to side as though someone were listening.

"I shall be the bait," he whispered. "My sword, Hrafnir,

cannot touch its foul green hide, and the horn of the Skrisung has no power over the beast, but you, Caltus Talienson, you and Sjonbrand, shall tonight bring an end to our curse.''

"Or at least we'll both die trying!" Cal grinned at the king, who was by now quite drunk on the mead.

"Right!" Hrafdi broke into laughter and slapped the boy soundly on the back.

They waited a while longer, till two of the three torches had gone out and Hrafdi had emptied his jug of mead. The king threw the container against the wall with a crash.

"Time to go!" he said, getting to his feet unsteadily and grabbing the last lit torch from the wall. Cal helped him out the door, and together they staggered along the deserted street between the silent houses. Hrafdi babbled on about the men and women who had lived in each of the darkened homes. It was a full hour before Cal managed to direct the wobbly monarch up the fateful path that ended at the door in the side of the great hall.

The king suddenly sobered up and fell silent. Cal opened the door ever so slightly and peered inside. He could see nothing, and he could not feel the creature's presence. Hrafdi growled, brushed the boy aside and kicked the door wide open. It crashed against a thick oaken post and the sound echoed across the deserted village. The light of the king's torch danced about the empty hall. The long table was littered with cups and mugs, and wooden chairs lay fallen along the sides.

"Come!" said the king. "I shall sit at the head of the table. Caltus, hide in the shadows behind me, under the great beams, and let us await the creature."

The boy shut the great door and dropped the iron latch in place, then made his way around the table and positioned himself behind a thick supporting post. Carved into the wood were intricate figures of boats and warriors, gods, giants, and trolls, all woven around a tree, at the base of which lurked a great serpent. The animals and other figures cut into the wood came alive in the flickering torchlight, a bit too alive to suit Cal. He grasped the hilt of Sjonbrand and a wave of reassurance and courage flowed through him.

The man and the boy then waited in ghostly silence for the horrible creature to come. Hrafdi's torch grew dim, flashed weakly, and went out. The still air in the hall now smelled of burnt oil and rags. For a time, Cal could see nothing at all, then his eyes adjusted to the faint moonlight that shone in through the two small windows at either end of the building.

The boy yawned noiselessly, his eyelids grew heavy, and he began to nod off to sleep, each time awakening with a jerk. Hrafdi, if he was still there, made no sound at all. Finally Cal wedged himself against the carved post and fell asleep standing up.

His rest was short lived, for Sjonbrand began to quiver at his waist and the gentle shaking brought the boy to wakefulness. He screwed up his nose, for the awful smell from the previous night was once again thick in the air. A scraping noise outside drew closer and Cal felt the evil presence of the beast near at hand. His heart beat faster and the boy tensed his body, preparing for the worst. Then he touched Sjonbrand again, and calm flooded his body. He could face anything now without fear; had not the Finngalkin told him as much earlier that very day?

A chorus of deep, nasty voices knifed through the dark silence:

> "Hrafdi, Grimnison, last of the Skrisung,
> Stand ready to meet your fate.

Tonight begins your journey
Beyond the river of death!''

The iron latch clacked and the door opened slowly. A dark shape obscured the moonlight that rushed in through the opening and one of the chairs by the door fell over.

"I await thee, monster!" spoke Hrafdi resolutely. "Yet the journey beyond the river of death tonight shall be thine own and not mine, I fear!"

Cal heard the king's chair scoot across the floor, and then the horn of the Skrisung sounded. It was a piercing blast that deafened the boy and shook the building to its very roots. Dirt and bits of straw tumbled down on Cal's shoulders and he watched as a portion of the roof gave way and crashed down upon the evil black shape that had entered the hall.

Eleven glowing yellow eyes suddenly glistened in the darkness, flashing with a brightness that did not come from the pale moonlight.

"You tease me, Hrafdi, with your foolish little trumpet," boomed the chorus of eleven voices. "It has been tried against me before to no avail." Twoscore and two arms lifted a huge beam that had fallen on the creature and tossed it aside as though it were but a twig. The object crashed against the far wall and the monster let out a horrific series of oaths in voices both high and low, each in a different language.

Hrafdi backed toward Cal and drew his sword, mumbling to himself, "Do not fail me, Hrafnir." The beast flipped the huge table over on its side with a fearsome crash and advanced menacingly on the king.

Caltus Talienson could wait no longer. Two hands went to the hilt and Sjonbrand floated out of the scabbard as if time were standing still. The blade gave off a blue-green light that filled the broken room, and the monster cowed, holding many of its arms over its eleven glowing eyes. A black rage filled the boy's heart and the blade whirled over his head, guiding his movements as he rushed forward to attack the beast.

His mind was no longer his own, and the boy heard himself uttering curses he had never learned. Before the monster could respond to this new threat, Cal was atop the accursed thing, hacking at its flailing arms, severing two of them from the body. Dark green blood gouted from the stumps and the monster shrieked eleven times over, reaching, grasping helplessly at its attacker, who always seemed a step ahead of its moves. Now Cal was behind it and Sjonbrand tore a horrible gash down the creature's scaly back, flaps of black flesh fell open and lumpy dark fluid drooled out in gobs onto the dirt floor of the hall.

The boy warrior dodged a deadly back swing from the beast's thick tail and circled around its hideous body. One swipe of the Runesword slashed across three eyes, popping them open as it passed. The beast lurched convulsively and jaws full of sharp teeth snapped at Cal, always too late. The beast wailed in frustration as each of its attacks fell short just as Cal moved on to hack and slash yet another portion of the hapless monster.

The ground was now slippery with the blood and entrails of the stricken monster, and Cal lost his footing and slid between its short stubby legs. Sjonbrand, with a will of its own, guided his arms in a deadly upward thrust that ripped open the gut of the beast. The monster's belly fell open and poured out a stinking mass of warm, black fluid, dark, bubbling slime, and pulsating organs.

Hrafdi, too, had joined the fray, and gone into a battle frenzy, slashing mercilessly at the monster with Hrafnir in hand, lopping off more arms and putting out yet another of the now fading eyes. Horrid shrieks and pitiful moans filled the hall, for the great monster, helpless against the vicious attacks of its foes, was sounding its own death rattle.

The fearful gurgles and screams carried across the land. Wolves in the forest heard it and began to howl and cry. Far away in her hut, Gertie, the Finngalkin, put a hand to her ear, cocked her strange-looking head to one side, and smiled to herself knowing that this night would see the end of the curse of the Skrisung.

The one-sided battle continued long into the morning, for the dreadful creature, though mortally wounded, would not yield, nor were Hrafdi or Cal likely to give it any quarter. Methodically the two chopped off the arms of the beast until nothing remained but a sickening forest of bloody stumps on the torn and mangled body. The king lunged forward and thrust Hrafnir deep into the great bulk, blinding its last remaining eye. Of the eleven voices only three remained, and they alternately cursed Hrafdi and shrieked miserably in pain.

Cal was dripping with the loathsome black fluid and green blood that issued from the beast, but it mattered not, for he was totally unaware of his physical surroundings. He had turned into a mindless instrument of destruction, guided by the force of will that lived within Sjonbrand. The great blade climbed into the air again and smashed down through the base of the monster's tail, its last remaining weapon. The huge appendage, fully three feet thick and seven feet long, fell to the dirt and rolled out the door, writhing and thrashing as it went, like the severed tail of a lizard.

Hrafdi let out a vengeful war cry as his blade plunged down a throat and silenced the last of the loathsome mouths.

"Never again will you summon a Skrisung to his death!" The king put his foot against the lifeless mouth of the beast and withdrew Hrafnir, which had wedged in bone. Cal finished the monster by chopping away at the short stubby legs. Soon the battered and slashed trunk of the beast crashed into the bloody sea that was the center of the meeting hall.

Still Hrafdi was not finished. His eyes wild with pent-up rage, the king climbed atop the lifeless carcass and hacked furiously at what remained, with each stroke calling out the names of those taken by the monster.

"Harald Gondulson! Uggh! And this is for Gerd! Daughter of Brising! Ungh! Neha! Infant child of Yngdyr! Urgh! And this is for my beloved wife, Svadlina!" Over and over again he smote the lifeless hulk, and bloody bits of the creature flew this way and that across the hall, splattering against the walls and floor and sometimes off Cal himself.

The boy shuddered. His arms were suddenly weak and a great weariness overcame him. He staggered back through the slippery muck and leaned, breathless, against the wall. Sjonbrand sheathed itself, his hands merely followed the hilt. All fire and energy faded from the boy as he slid limply to the floor. He sat there unable to move and watched, unseeing, as the king of the Skrisung recited the roll of the dead and methodically chopped and slashed at what was left of the monster.

Hrafdi did not stop till his voice was gone and he had delivered the last blow, naming his father, King Grimni, who had perished at the hands of the monster the previous night. He could utter no further oaths nor lift Hrafnir for another stroke. In his fury, the angry king had chopped the hated creature to bits.

The floor of the great hall was covered with a thick layer of black ooze and shredded pieces of monster, and what walls still stood were spattered with blood and gruesome chunks of flesh. The only part of the enemy that remained intact was the beast's tail, which had rolled out of the hall after being severed by Caltus.

Hrafdi staggered sideways, knee-deep in the mess, and surveyed the carnage. He took a deep breath, put away his sword and began to struggle slowly through the sea of slippery debris to where Cal sat.

"We've done it!" he whispered hoarsely, leaning over and extending a hand to the weary boy. Cal looked at the king, reached up, and instead of being lifted, pulled Hrafdi down by his side.

"What a fight!"

"Revenge!"

Covered from head to toe with the blood and guts of the beast, oblivious to the dreadful stench, the two exhausted warriors sat against the wall, unable to move.

CHAPTER
17

Elizebith spent the remainder of the day seated on her cushion, studying the two amber balls. More and more she was convinced that they had had everything to do with her unusual composure and her ability to turn the tables on Schlein. She wondered what else they might be able to do. Closing her eyes and curling her fingers around the stones, she concentrated her thoughts and tried to cast a simple spell. For a moment, it seemed that it would work; Bith could feel the spell hovering on the edge of existence, but then the feeling dissipated and so did the spell.

Bith should have been discouraged, but she wasn't, for the spell had almost worked. If she could only get out of this room, maybe she could reclaim her powers. It was an exciting thought.

Her thoughts turned to Schlein and his injuries. She wondered what form his revenge would take. There was no sense in hoping that he would forget about it. She could only hope that he would not harm her unknown accomplice, for with his help she might survive whatever horror Schlein might visit upon her.

These and other grim thoughts occupied Bith throughout the long day and the night that followed. There was no bread and no water, no eyes at the door, no sound upon the steps, no murmur from the castle below. It was as though she were disconnected from all else, floating on a plane of existence somewhere beyond the mortal world.

It was also lonely. As night fell and the darkness within became as dark as that outside the shuttered window, Bith found herself listening more closely than ever, waiting anxiously for the silent footfall on the stair. Waiting for her unknown friend.

Brightfeather watched anxiously beneath the sweep of the overhanging bushes that had sheltered her ever since her wing had been injured. The orange-red spread of color that was the sun filled her eyes with a great burst of light and then slipped beneath the dark edge of the horizon as smoothly and slickly as a fish through water.

The little bird's heart thudded against her ribs as she thought again of the hawk who had so nearly ended her life. She would not face the hawk this night, for the hawk was but an extension of the huge four-legged man and, Thistle had assured her, the two of them only ventured out when the sun was high.

Brightfeather shivered again, as any self-respecting bird should do, thinking of the dangers that she would soon face. Owls. And night-flying swiftwings and eagles and griffins and who knew what else! Night was the time for gathering in the safety of numbers in bushes or trees and hiding till the light of day. Night was the time for predators and danger and death.

Brightfeather did not want to leave the safety of the bush. Nor did she wish to fly up into the darkness of the night, higher than a mere sparrow was ever meant to fly. Her wing was barely mended and she did not know if she would be strong enough to succeed. More than anything she wished herself back in her favorite tree, on her favorite perch, surrounded by the twittering warmth of friends and family with her head tucked beneath her wing.

But there was the problem of the parchment, the tiny scroll still tied to her ankle with a bit of filmy thread that had resisted all efforts of her sharp beak to separate it from her leg. And even more so was the strange compulsion to do that which she most feared, fly to the tower and deliver the scrap of paper to the one who resided within.

It was the little man who was the root of all her problems. Brightfeather resolved to avoid people for as long as she might live, if she were fortunate enough to live just one night longer. She heard Thistle, Flashtail, Whitewing, and Flax Seed talking among themselves, somewhere above her, and felt better. She was not totally alone, for they would fly with her, no matter what perils she must face.

There was no sense putting the thing off any longer. What was to be done was best done now. Brightfeather's tiny beak quivered and her throat swelled with air as she puffed herself up.

"Here I come!" she warbled. Then, with a single burst of energy that flung her out of the bushes with a furious explosion of feathers, she launched herself into the darkness. All around her there were similar flashes of feathers, and wheeling into a tight turn, Brightfeather and her companions rose toward the distant tower.

Ormoc sat in his chambers, crouched before a single dim candle, twisting his hands and worrying about what was to become of him . . . and of the girl, Bith. Just the thought of her set his heart pounding and he called forth the memory of the flow of her dark hair and the exact color of her unusual eyes. Something about her touched his heart in a way that it had not been touched for many a long year.

It made Ormoc remember what it had been like in the sunrise of his youth, when he was still young enough to have dreams, before he had lost his soul and his hope to the likes of Schlein and the Dark Lord. There had even been a girl once, a girl with clear eyes and hair as sleek as nightfall, who had loved him.

Another evil lord, one whose name no longer mattered, for the world always seemed to abound with masters of evil, had caused the girl to die and Ormoc, too young and too terrified and too filled with the knowledge of his own vulnerability, had failed to save her. He had never forgiven himself. Somehow, helping Bith had helped to erase a small measure of that harbored grief.

Things had been very quiet in the tower since the startling events of the morning. Ormoc's thin lips twisted into the semblance of a smile. What he wouldn't have given to have been there, to have seen Schlein humiliated! Even the thought was exhilarating, and for the first time, as though he were looking into his own crystal globe, Ormoc realized the true depth of his hatred for the wretched Schlein!

The quiet that cloaked the place was not a peaceful silence but one that fairly reeked of fear as the inhabitants huddled down to ride out the whirlwind of fury that was certain to come. Ormoc himself had been ordered to find Murcroft, who had the good fortune of being abroad during the crisis, and now could not be found. Ormoc was to bring him back by any means.

Schlein had been closeted with Tellarko ever since the incident, and the terrified wizard had come and gone numerous times, fetching bandages and healing ointments, and even Ormoc's cabinets had been plundered for the ingredients of a healing spell. But the single necessary item had been missing from each and every supply in the castle. Nothing had been found except ample piles of rat scats where the herbs had once been. Which was extremely odd in itself.

Rats were plentiful in this castle as in every castle, but they usually had the good sense to show little evidence of themselves. This time it almost seemed that they had stolen the herbs and left their signature! But such a thought was foolishness. Ormoc almost chuckled at the thought. Rat signatures! Tellarko had complained bitterly. Surely it was a sign of senility!

He had gone to the kitchen to try to find Bith something to eat, but the kitchen was barred from within and he could hear the cook and his helpers sniveling, no doubt in fear of their own pathetic lives.

Next he had gone to Schlein's quarters to see if there was anything which could be salvaged, but the entire room had been consumed by fire and there was nothing left of any value. Even now, tiny flickers of flame sprouted here and there in lazy spirals and the acrid smell of smoke hung heavy in his nostrils.

He turned as though to go down the stairs, thinking that he might comfort Bith with his presence, even though he had naught to offer her. Ormoc stopped in his tracks and his heart lurched within his chest. There was Schlein, leaning against the doorjamb, with Tellarko trembling behind him.

"Ah, yes, my good, faithful servant, Ormoc," Schlein said, peering at scryer with bright, feverish eyes. "Come to offer me comfort, have you?"

"No, lord, uh, I mean, yes, of course, to offer my condolences for your illness," said Ormoc, doing his best to hide his fear and his horror at Schlein's appearance.

Schlein's face was raw and leaking fluid from a multitude

of fissures. It was as though the very flesh had tried to melt off his bones. And nearly succeeded. The flesh was puffy and proud and red and angry looking. If and when it healed, it would scar, that much was certain. Schlein might be disfigured for life. Not that he had been anything beautiful to see before. The Exalted Master would be as hideous outside as his soul was inside.

"Condolences, ehh?" grunted Schlein, a dry chuckle slipping from his charred lips. "Condolences are good, Ormoc, but flannel mullein would have been better. I don't suppose you know what happened to every single vial of flannel mullein in the tower, do you?"

"I, sir?" Ormoc's brow furrowed in surprise. "Why would I know anything about such a thing, Exalted Master?"

"Oh, I don't know, Ormoc. It seems that there are a lot of things going on around here lately that can't be explained. I thought that maybe you, with your crystal vision, might have a few answers for me. Or is there some other reason why I would have a scryer in my employ?"

"Sir?" Ormoc said, wanting to take a step backward, yet knowing that he must not show fear if he had any hope of living.

"Things have been disappearing, Ormoc," said Schlein as he advanced toward the frightened scryer. "The cooks tell me that food and wine have been vanishing on a regular basis. The steward reports that cushions and linens and coverlets are missing from the cabinets. My own room was rifled and my amber stones spirited away. Today the prisoner, a mere girl, succeeds in destroying these chambers and causing me bodily harm. . . ."

"And now it is found that the prime ingredient necessary for a cure spell is missing, causing me untold anguish. I do not like pain, Ormoc. I cause pain! It has been a long time since anyone succeeded in hurting me. I had forgotten what pain felt like. Now I remember and I do not like it.''

The huge man edged closer to his scryer. "You offer me condolences and yet you have seen nothing unusual about the goings on in this tower . . . and you still have no idea what happened to the girl's companions?" Tellarko was standing behind his master, pointing an accusing finger at Ormoc, trying to look as important as possible.

"What about you, Ormoc?" boomed Schlein. "How do you feel about pain?"

The scryer opened his mouth, which was suddenly very dry, to speak, to defend himself, when he was seized by the most awful pain he had ever felt in his entire life. It felt as though someone had wrapped him from head to toe in a single thread of burning pain. It was all but unendurable.

"Ah, cat must have your tongue," said Schlein as he smiled gently, almost beneficently at the tormented scryer.

Ormoc felt the bands of pain slacken and then fall away, although he could feel them hovering just beyond his body.

"Well, scryer, what do you know of these incidents?" Schlein asked a bit more forcibly. "You will tell me what you know and give me the flannel mullein that I need."

Schlein grabbed an unbroken cup from the table and crushed it to shards with his hand. "If you do so, I may still be convinced to spare your miserable life."

Ormoc opened his mouth to speak, to remind Schlein of all that his faithful servant had done for his Exalted Master. To convince him that he had nothing to do with the missing herbs. To save his very life, which seemed to be hanging in the balance . . . but then something stopped him and the scryer defiantly closed his mouth and his eyes and shook his head.

"Ah, Ormoc, Ormoc, what is this? Developing a spine

after all these years? I think you will find it a luxury you cannot afford.''

Once again the fiery bands of pain wrapped themselves around Ormoc and began to tighten, only this time there were more of them than before.

It took the scryer many hours to die. But his iron resolve lasted to the end and he told Schlein nothing at all. And in the last hours before dawn, the pain picked him up and carried him away on a wave that was pure feeling, neither bad nor good, just a solid wave of feeling. Ormoc knew, in some tiny portion of his brain, that it simply meant that his poor tortured body could tolerate no more.

As he drifted away on the wave, shutting out the sound of Schlein's ranting, a soft bright glow began to shine at the edge of his vision. He separated himself from the heavy remains of his earthly body and gave in to the wondrous feeling, the end of the pain, welcoming it with all his heart. And as he drifted closer to the light, it seemed to him that he could see the slender, graceful figure of a woman standing at the edge of the bright cloud and beckoning to him, opening her arms wide as though to greet him.

He found that he could stand, that his body was younger and slimmer and lighter than it had been in years, and that it was free of the evil that had surrounded him for so long. He ran toward the woman, for he felt in his heart that he knew her, and as the light enveloped him with a warm caress and the joy of homecoming, he knew that it was she whom he had loved so long ago and that he was now and had always been . . . forgiven.

Bith awakened on her cushions in the middle of the night, which seemed somehow blacker than usual, and was filled with a deep feeling of sadness. A bad dream, perhaps. The girl looked around carefully, nothing appeared to be amiss. She took the last sip of water from her crystal goblet and lay back down to sleep.

CHAPTER
18

A brilliant flash of lightning and a resounding thunderclap startled Cal into wakefulness. He was still in a daze from the recent battle and was only partially conscious as a torrent of rain began to descend through the broken roof of the building. The cool rain felt good and the fresh smell cleared away the stench of death that had filled the place. The boy's eyes suddenly opened wide with amazement as ghostly figures appeared in the hall, shimmering in the rainy darkness between the lightning flashes.

He nudged Hrafdi with his elbow. The sleeping king snorted and then let out a yelp when he too saw the glowing apparitions. The strangely luminous forms of warriors, women, and children hurried busily about, sweeping the grisly remains of the beast from the ruined hall.

"The Skrisung!" murmured an awe-struck Hrafdi. "They have come back!" Cal could feel the man tremble with excitement. The ghosts, however, took no notice of the two warriors slumped against the wall. As the drenching rain poured into the hall, the apparitions used the water to good purpose as they mopped, pushed, picked, and wiped away all traces of the beast. The work went on amid the crash and roll of the thunderstorm until, at last, all signs of the battle had been cleared away.

The apparitions then formed a double line by the door and several ghostly warriors walked in with the severed tail of the monster. They carried it down the hall to the wall behind the king's chair. Spikes were driven into the timber, and a great chain pulled the thing up to a place of honor. The trophy of the Skrisung would hang there for all who came after to see.

Hrafdi was on his feet clapping loudly at this, but the ghosts were not through. The larger men set themselves to lifting the timbers felled by the horn, hefting the thick beams easily and floating them gently into place through the pouring rain. Others gathered the broken sections of the roof and soon the rain pattered against the roof and the great hall was restored.

Hrafdi had tears in his eyes as each of the ghosts paraded slowly past him. They wore expressions of happiness and calm. The sad king reached out to touch the glimmering forms, but his hand passed through their ethereal bodies and they walked on. Hrafdi pointed out friends, relations and King Grimni to Cal, and waved at each of them and smiled as the parade marched by. Last of all came the iridescent form of an exceptionally beautiful woman with long braids of golden hair. She stopped before them and the king dropped to his knees, clasping his hands in front of his lips, sobbing.

"Svadlina, my dearest love . . . stay with me!"

The ghost spoke in a gentle whisper, extending her soft arm to her husband's hands. "We must go now, Hrafdi Grimnison, my husband. Know that I shall always love you. We shall all rest easy knowing that you have avenged us."

She turned to face Cal, who stood incredulous at the

king's side. "Would that the gods have delivered you unto us sooner, Caltus Talienson. We thank you." A warm peaceful glow flowed through the boy's body as her hand passed through his. "Hrafdi will reward you!"

Svadlina's image again spoke to her husband. "There is hope, yet, in your world for the Skrisung, my husband. For we will go forth and call back those of us who left us to live among others. The Skrisung will return to their village, and they will bring their wives and husbands and their children . . . This will be their home and you shall be their king!"

So saying, she turned and silently walked across the hall, her body passing through the table, and then disappeared into the wall, and the great hall of the Skrisung fell dark. The rain let up and soon stopped entirely and Cal noticed a finger of blue daylight as I poked its way through the small windows. Hrafdi came to life then, staggered to the door and threw it open.

"Come, Caltus, we have a victory celebration to organize!" The boy followed the king and they walked back to Hrafdi's house in the half light of early morning. The clouds overhead boiled away and before the two had reached the low door, the sky was clear, full of stars on one half and glowing with dawn on the other.

Hrafdi stopped and took a deep breath of the clean cool air. "For the first time in a long time the stench of death has gone from my village!"

The king pulled a small cart out of a broken-down shed beside his house, wheeled it to the door, and then led Cal inside. Together they filled the cart with several jugs of mead, a number of wooden boxes and chests. When Cal questioned him as to the contents, Hrafdi smiled and refused to say anything. Soon the load was complete and the two pushed the heavily laden cart back through the deserted street, up the hill and into the great hall. The king produced some torches, lit them and stuck them in cressets along the walls while Cal set the jugs and boxes on the table.

Hrafdi opened one of the chests and took from it two gold mugs, which he quickly filled to overflowing with the thick mead. He handed one to Cal.

"A toast, Caltus Talienson, to our marvelous victory over the beast of the Skrisung!" Cal smiled, and took the drink.

"To our victory . . . and to the memory!"

Their vessels clanked together as they stared up at the tail of the beast, which hung on the wall above them. The drink had lost none of its strength and burned as it went down, but this time Cal had something to celebrate and welcomed the strong brew. He had a Runesword by his side, and would soon be off to rescue Bith. He could afford to rejoice. The boy emptied his mug before the king had even finished his.

After downing two more pints of the potent liquid, Cal plopped down in a chair, laughing. The king filled the mugs again, and then opened one of the chests.

" 'Tis time I rewarded you for your deeds!"

"No, no, Hrafdi," protested Cal. "Your happiness and the death of the monster is all the reward I need!"

The king shook his head gravely. "You heard the words of my queen! You shall be richly rewarded!" Out of the chest came two gold bracelets. He snapped them shut around the boy's wrists. "Ah, a perfect fit! It is said that these impart strength to the bearer, if his cause be just!"

Cal twisted his arm back and forth, examining the objects. They were covered with ornate carvings and, come to think of it, his arms did feel a little different. He slammed a fist down on the table with a resounding band and the jugs, mugs, and boxes bounced visibly.

"See what I mean?" beamed the king. They downed

their mead and Hrafdi handed Cal a bag of gold coins. They could not be refused. More mead was drunk and then the boy became the recipient of a fine round shield, seemingly made of gold, yet light in feel and easy to balance.

"I . . . I can't take this. It's too much!"

"Silence! That is only the beginning," admonished the king, who poured their cups full once again and then dug even deeper into the chest. The gifts kept coming and the mead kept flowing as the morning wore on. They made repeated trips to the great latrine behind the hall. It had twelve stalls, one for each of the elders. Cal was allowed to use the king's own.

By noon neither one of them could rise from their chairs, and Hrafdi's speech was slurring heavily. It mattered little though, for everything he said was tremendously funny and Cal and the king both laughed till their sides ached. By now Cal had been weighted down with countless rings and gems, jewels, crowns, bags of gold, a necklace, a golden helm, the shield and more, and he doubted he would be able to stand, even if he were sober.

The celebration continued for the rest of the day and on into the night. Though the drink continued to flow, Cal remained conscious and the slow speeches of the king remained laden with great humor. At midnight they struggled to their feet and drank one last toast, to the beast, whose tail hung ominously above them in the light of the last torch. It seemed to Cal as though the thing twitched at that very moment, but he couldn't be sure. Hrafdi then fell back into his chair and began to snore.

Then Cal too collapsed in a heap, sprawled out across a chair with his arms and head on the table.

Came the morn, Cal was surprised and relieved to feel well and refreshed as he awoke. He had been certain the night before that he would regret all the mead he had consumed. The king sat across from him, smiling.

"There's magic in this place! Do you not feel better today?"

"Wonderful," said Cal, stretching luxuriously. "But now, Hrafdi, I must be off. I have stayed too long as it is, for the lives of my friends are in peril."

"Then there is one last gift I must bestow upon you before you depart." The king arose and crossed the hall. There on the wall, where the ghosts had placed it, hung the horn of the Skrisung. Hrafdi lovingly pulled it down and carried it over to the boy. "Sound this in battle and it will serve you as it has served us!"

"Oh no, not that!" Cal pleaded. "It is too valuable."

The king shook his head, and the two argued for a while, and finally settled the matter. Cal agreed to take the bracelets, the horn, the helm, and the shield, for they all suited a warrior. The gold, jewelry, and gems he left behind. The Skrisung, as Cal pointed out, would soon be returning from afar, and their king would need a treasury to build anew.

They walked arm in arm across the village, Cal's helm glinting brilliantly in the sunlight. At last they came to the edge of the forest and stopped for the final parting.

"Farewell, Caltus Talienson, thank you for all you have done. If ever you return to Northunderland and the realm of the Skrisung know that you have a place at the hearth, for your name shall be remembered by us always."

"I must come back and bring my companions!"

"They, too, are welcome," Hrafdi offered with a warm smile.

Cal shook the king's outstretched hand, and then the two embraced. They stood silently facing each other for a moment and then the boy adjusted his pack, turned on his heel and marched off into the wood.

• • •

Gunnar Greybeard paced nervously back and forth in the sand, muttering under his breath. It had been two days. The boy had had more than enough time to gather the sword and slay the monster—and where was that troll? Would Lennia and her women ever let go of their treasure?

"I should never have left them on their own!" he wailed. But it had been nice to see Glasvellir Hall once again, and where Cal and Hathor had gone he would have been but useless baggage. Then a voice hailed him from atop the cliff. He looked up. It was Cal, wearing a golden helm. At the same time a group of troll women came out of the cleft in the rock, carrying a limp Hathor between them. They struggled over to where the amused dwarf stood and dropped their helpless load at his feet.

"Here, Greybeard, is your troll," Lennia said with a broad grin on her face. She rubbed her bare belly with her hand and chuckled along with the others. "The future of the trolls of Auseviget and Northunderland has been secured. Though I fear this one will be of no use to you for a few days."

Greybeard smiled, pulling at his beard, and Hathor lifted his head weakly and looked at him. A satisfied grin crossed his broad face and then his red locks thumped back down onto the beach.

"Well, I can imagine, foster mother! It looks as though I am about to have some new foster kin!"

It was all Caltus could do, even with his bracelets of strength and what help Greybeard mustered, to roll the troll up over the rail and back into *Skidbladner*. At last the mighty task was done, however, and the ship pulled out from the beach. Cal tucked a blanket under Hathor's head and then dug into his pack for a precious item he'd been saving for a moment like this.

Just as the winds came up and *Skidbladners'* red-and-white-striped sail popped open, a green flag, emblazoned with an eagle carrying a fish, rose to the top of the mast and flapped noisily in the breeze.

Cal leaned back and looked up at it with pride. Greybeard appeared at his side, looking at him quizzically.

"My father's flag," Cal said quietly.

"I'm certain he would be proud of you now," answered the dwarf.

CHAPTER
19

Brightfeather struggled upward into the dark night, her eyes fixed on the small square of deeper darkness set into the wall of the tower that was her destination. It seemed so very far away, so very high, an almost impossible goal for one so small, but she had been pledged to carry out the mission and so she would, or die in the effort. Which also seemed quite possible.

All around her she could sense the rise and fall of other wings, the straining of other hearts, the shared fears of her companions, Thistle, Flax Seed, Flashtail, Whitewing, and now many others as well, summoned from the surrounding countryside, who lent her their courage as well as their presence.

The tiny winged contingent rose higher and higher in the inky night sky, rising above the first level of the tower, which echoed with orcan laughter and whose windows shed golden light across the black moat, then above the second and third levels, dark, without the tiniest thread of light. Just below the fourth level, Brightfeather sensed rather than heard approaching danger and banked to the left. A swift current of air sliced alongside her, tumbling the tiny messenger off course. She darted away in terror as quickly as she could regain her balance, beak open, heart pounding against her rib cage so loudly that she thought it must be heard. Sparing a moment's glance upward, her pounding heart nearly stopped, for there, suspended above her, talons curved, wings swept back, cruel beak opened wide, was a great horned owl, so huge as to blot out the moon!

Brightfeather swerved without thinking and slammed into the wall of the tower itself, stunning herself and nearly tumbling head over heels into the dark, still moat, waiting below. Had she fallen, it would have meant her death. The great owl was waiting for her to reappear, but Brightfeather's tiny claws curled around the thick mat of ivy, which clung like a carpet to the tower, and hung on for dear life.

The owl circled for long moments, unable to discern the whereabouts of its prey. At last the night hunter, unwilling to wait any longer for the tiny sparrow who would be no more than a mouthful at best, winged over in a graceful dive and sped silently away toward the forest in search of larger, more substantial prey.

Slowly, Brightfeather's breathing returned to normal and her heart stopped its frantic pounding. As she gripped the thick ivy, she heard the worried twitters of her many companions emerging from the dense leaf cover that had shielded them all from the deadly predator.

"Brightfeather, sister friend. Do you live?" came the query from Whitewing.

"I am here," chirped Brightfeather. "I am safe. Who lives?" she asked, unable to ask whether any had been taken by the owl.

There followed a sort of twittering roll call of all present, as each bird sounded off, almost all at the same time. Suddenly a shadowy form leaned out a nearby window to see what was making all the racket and the birds fell silent. The intruder shook his head and disappeared back into the tower, and the birds resumed their chatter.

"All live," came the welcome reply, and Brightfeather felt the tension drain out of her small body. She turned one eye to the dark night and scanned it for sign of danger, knowing that she had best be on her way before the owl or another of its equally dangerous relatives returned. Yet she was not able to force herself to leave the safety of the ivy for the dangers of the open night. Many fangs and beaks and claws were waiting out there to rip and shred her tiny body. But the parchment bound to her leg, and a promise she had made, commanded that she do just that.

And then, torn by fear and indecision, an idea came to her. A wondrous idea! Turning her head upward, she gripped a strand of ivy with her beak and, finding a foothold on which to lever her body forward, she crept upward through the dense green foliage.

"Come! Come! Follow me!" she warbled happily, knowing that she had found the means whereby she and her companions might reach the distant goal in safety. It was unbirdlike, to be sure, quite foreign to their nature, but life was far more important than appearances, and for the moment, that was all that really mattered. Soon the entire band of tiny birds was hopping and climbing, unseen, up the side of Murcroft's tower under the cover of a forest of clinging vines.

Meanwhile, halfway up the tower, Schlein paced back and forth in his new personal chambers, locked deep in a fierce, black rage and still wrapped in pain which he had not experienced in many a long year. It was a most unpleasant feeling and one which he planned to share with as many unwilling recipients as possible. He had slipped up and finished with Ormoc too soon. It was time to deal with Elizebith, wretched uncooperative daughter of Morea, but he would have to be more careful.

Schlein paced in darkness because light hurt his swollen, blistered eyes. But he did not need light to think his dark thoughts, and he pondered his plans as he strode back and forth over the uneven flagstones.

The massive man cursed out loud, swinging his fist wildly in the dark. Ormoc had escaped him, escaped into the safety and distance of death, beyond even Schlein's grasp. And he had succeeded in dying without revealing anything about his part in the girl's rebellion . . . if he, in fact, had had anything to do with it. Schlein was not even certain that it was so. For all he knew, he had slain one of his most valuable servants for nothing, losing the only scryer available to him. Now he would have little or no chance of finding Elizebith's missing companions and learning what they were up to, or of locating Murcroft, whose absence was most annoying.

Tellarko was gone, out of the tower, searching for the flannel mullein, the single missing ingredient that would allow him to cast a healing spell on his wounds. But even the spell would not save him from the scarring that was sure to occur due to the length of time that had elapsed since the initial injury. Schlein was vain about what he viewed as his own brand of good looks and he resented their being marred.

Back and forth he paced, wondering how he could force the dark-haired beauty to reveal the whereabouts of her companions as well as give in to his demands. Strangely enough, he seemed to want her even more since the incident in the tower, rather than less. A part of him admired her courage, even though he himself had paid its price. He stopped for a moment and smiled to himself. What a wife she would make! With her at his side he might even be able to challenge the power of the Dark Lord himself.

An odd rustling noise outside the window drew him and he peered out, wondering what it might be. An owl winged away toward the distant forest, its form silhouetted against the rising moon, but there was nothing else to be seen. A tiny shiver seemed to run through the ivy beside him and he thought at first that it might be the wind, but even the wind was silent. Sibilant squeaks and warbles could be heard among the dense cover of leaves and Schlein shrugged as he pulled his head back inside the room. Rats, he thought, too many damn rats in this tower, both inside and out. Murcroft would have to do something about them when he returned. And eliminating the noise from his thoughts, he returned to his pacing.

Blackwhiskers had not found his task to be an easy one. Unlike their country cousins, the tower rats had little interest in helping the imprisoned humans and their foul orc servants. Schlein was human, as was Murcroft, and those two had done nothing to endear themselves to the rats. On the many occasions that rats and humans or orcs had come into contact, pain and death had been the result . . . for the rats, that is.

In vain did Blackwhiskers attempt to convince his cousins that some of the humans were different, and only the fact that he was family caused them to endure his efforts at persuasion. Finally, a large grey rat named He-Who-Scales-Walls, but more commonly known as Wallclimber, the leader of the tower rats, grew tired of Blackwhiskers' entreaties.

"Look, you probably believe what yer sayin', but you don't really know these large ones. They ain't to be trusted. They're all sneaky-like. They says one thing and does another. They're always lookin' fer a chance to kill each other

off an' take the other guy's stuff fer themselves. They ain't
a bit honorable like us rats. Ya' can't trust 'em, take it from
me.''

"My friends are different, honest!" said Blackwhiskers,
growing more and more agitated as his efforts fell on deaf
ears. "They ain't tryin' to do nothin' fer themselves. All
they wants to do is rescue that girl up in the tower, and if
we help 'em they give me their word to see that things are
better fer us rats!"

"Ha! How would they do that?" sneered Wallclimber,
his interest piqued in spite of himself.

"They say that all the orcs'll be gone. An' the evil ones
an' the hawk too. An' they say they'll do whatever else
they can to make it a better place for us to live. They give
me their word.''

"Pah, a human's word ain't worth spit," said Wallclimber, hawking and spitting on the ground to emphasize his
words.

"One of them is an elf!" corrected Blackwhiskers.

"Same difference! What would they want us to do, anyways?"

"Fun stuff," answered the country rat from Shadowvale
Cave. "We gotta fool and confuse the orcs and get 'em to
fight amongst themselves. We gotta chew our way through
some wooden doors, and raid the kitchen and pantry, stealing food, and trashin' the place—stuff like that!"

"Hmm, that could be fun, but we rats do all that kind
of stuff already.''

"Not like this! We gotta take this place apart!"

He-Who-Scales-Walls sat for a moment preening his
whiskers. "All right," he murmured, as he pondered Blackwhiskers' words. "Foolin' orcs is easy to do, them bein'
so dumb an' all. Chewin' wood is no big deal an' eatin'
food is downright pleasant. All right, Blackie, you can count

on me, but the others'll have to speak fer themselves.''

The others, all four hundred and seventy odd, had only been waiting for Wallclimber to make his decision, for despite his casual words, none of them would have dared to oppose him. Now they added their own squeaks of acceptance to those of their leader.

''Great!'' squealed Blackwhiskers, his tail thrashing with excitement, glad that they had agreed for eating the castle's entire supply of flannel mullein by himself had been enough to convince him that he needed help. ''Now this is what we gots to do!'' The leaders of the various rat factions came forward and formed a planning committee. Crowding in among them, the rat from Shadowvale Cave told them of Endril's plan.

Bith sat awake in her room, unable to get back to sleep, staring into the darkness, knowing in her heart that something was very, very wrong. It had not been a bad dream that had awakened her earlier, but something far, far worse. The tiny spark of hope that had buoyed her through this awful imprisonment seemed to have been extinguished and her heart lay heavy and leaden within her breast.

She sighed deeply and cradled her head on her arms, wondering where her friends were now and wishing with all her heart that she were with them. She could not help but wonder if she would ever see them again. Never had she felt so helpless, so completely lost, so utterly alone. Even a visitation from Vili would have been welcomed.

There had been no further summons from Schlein. His hated visage had not appeared in the slot in the door. Nor had she received her daily allotment of stale bread and water. Worst of all, her unknown friend, ever in her thoughts, was most noticeable by his very absence. He should have visited her by now. She prayed that no harm had come to him, but his absence was not a good omen.

Bith wanted not for food or drink as there was still a goodly amount of wine left together with a round of cheese and a bit of smoked ham, but Bith felt no stirrings of thirst or hunger and passed the time worrying about those who had cared for her.

As the blackness of night turned to the paleness of early dawn, Bith was startled to hear a key turn in the lock, and for a brief moment she dared to hope that her anonymous friend had returned to free her. She jumped to her feet and stood before the door, wringing her hands, her heart thumping hard against her ribs. But terror and dismay replaced her desperate hopes as Schlein's evil countenance appeared in the narrow opening.

Bith gasped as the grey light of the approaching dawn revealed the damage she had wrought. Schlein's face and upper body were a suppurating mass of oozing, blistered flesh. His features were all but obliterated by the raw, seeping wounds, and his nose and eyes and mouth appeared as dark caverns unto his black soul. His eyes burned with a feverish intensity, and as he edged into the room he was preceded by the stink of charred flesh. Behind him lurked two burly guards, who stood blocking the door. Schlein fastened his gaze on the terrified girl, yet spoke not a word and did not look away.

Bith was transfixed with horror, by the knowledge of what she had done and at the thought of his revenge. Gone was her earlier semblance of courage, and all but overwhelmed by her fear she failed to think of the amber stones, now tucked away in her pocket where they could do her little good, for they required the warmth of human touch to release their subtle powers.

Schlein's silence was more terrifying than anything he

could have said, and he advanced into the room, his gaze still locked on Bith, who retreated two steps for his every one.

Only when the evil man had reached the center of the room and Bith was pressed against the far wall did he glance around him. His damaged eyes took in the sight of the luxuries hidden in the small alcove. He nodded once as though confirming some inner thought and turned to the guards at the door.

"Get this trash out of here!" he ordered, pointing at Bith's treasures. The two men came forward with a large canvas bag and filled it with all the booty that Ormoc had brought. Then, tying it securely, they hefted the bag between them and quickly left the room.

Bith crouched below the single window, as far from Schlein as the tiny room would allow. The door was now unguarded, but Bith could not even contemplate escape, for Schlein's presence filled the place with emanations of his dark power and robbed her of what little strength she had managed to acquire. Now she was certain that her friend had met with death at Schlein's hands, for he had seemed certain of what he would find. If he allowed her to live, she would truly be alone.

Schlein glowered at her although his look seemed to hold no indication of anger, but rather a sense of ownership. "Tomorrow," he whispered, "tomorrow you will be my bride." And leaving her with that single fearful thought, he turned and exited, closing the door and locking it behind him.

There had been no rage, no murderous outburst, not even a threat or a slammed door, and that more than anything filled Bith with terror. Something must have happened. Something truly awful. Mayhaps Schlein had apprehended her companions and slain them. Could he and Murcroft have succeeded in bringing the Mistwall to these lands and driven all that was good and right out of all the world? Was all hope dead, and would she now be forced to be the bride of that despicable villain and see her powers drained to enhance his evil?

Overcome by those horrid thoughts Bith collapsed in a heap beneath the window in what was left of her pile of straw and began to weep, wondering how she might kill herself, for hateful as that thought might be, becoming Schlein's bride was a fate much worse than death.

The sound of her weeping filled the small room, all but obliterating a soft, persistent rustle that came from outside the tiny window. Twitters and cheeps began to compete with Bith's sobs, and some corner of her mind registered the fact that dawn had come. But birds had never dared to visit the tower before and the very inconsistency tugged at her mind, begging for her attention.

Lifting her head, Bith turned her tear-streaked face toward the window and saw, outlined against the pink and grey streaks of dawn, a small bird, almost inconsequential in its very ordinariness. Ordinary in the extreme, with dull brown plumage. Ordinary in every way except that the bird had tilted its little head and was looking at her. It chirped loudly and held up one of its feet. A tiny bit of parchment was fastened to its leg.

Scarcely daring to hope, Bith reached out with trembling hand and held her breath as the little bird shivered once and then hopped boldly upon her outstretched finger.

Bith saw the bright gleam of its eye as she drew it near and the flutter of its heart as it beat against the fluff of its breast, and she knew its terror as she had known her own.

"Do not be afraid, little one," she whispered, smoothing the bird's feathers with her finger. "I will not hurt you." The bird calmed visibly, as though recognizing the intent of her words even if it could not decipher them, and carefully, so as not to alarm it further, she pulled the single silken strand that held the parchment, allowing it to fall free.

The bird shook its leg and stretched it backward as though glad to be free of its burden and then, cocking its head to one side, listened as she spoke, its bright eyes fixed upon her own.

Still holding the tiny creature, Bith spread the bit of parchment wide between two fingers and read the words:

> "Do not despair, we are with you, and shall
> soon return."

It was signed by Cal's own hand. Joy and happiness filled Bith, driving despair from her like sunshine banishing shadows. "Oh, bird, what happiness you have brought me in my hour of need," she whispered, tears again welling in her eyes. "Surely, you have saved me from a fearsome and foolish death. Knowing that my friends are near, I will have the courage to withstand even the Dark Lord himself."

She lifted the sparrow close to her face. "Dear bird, I have not the words to thank you, but if you will wait, I will send a reply to he who sent this missive and mayhaps he will find an appropriate reward."

Bith turned back to the room, searching for something to use as a marker, and then felt the weight of claws lift from her finger. She heard the flutter of wings and looked back in time to see the small bird vanish out the window.

"Wait!" cried Bith, "come back!" thinking perhaps that the bird had misunderstood. But even as she watched, clutching the bars in her hands, the small flock of sparrows wheeled up into the rising dawn and then fled straight as an arrow for the distant fields. The girl knew that there was no hope that they would return.

"May the gods go with you and protect you always," Bith called after their fleeing forms, and she could but hope that it would be so.

But there had been no misunderstanding. Brightfeather had understood Bith's words all too well and had fled because of them, having no desire to find herself trapped in another desperate mission. The bird's only desire was to return to the safety of her own world from which she would never again stray.

As the winged messenger darted away through the cold morning air, surrounded by those loyal and stout-hearted friends, Bith's words were carried to her by some trick of the winds and she felt herself enveloped in a cocoon of momentary warmth. Unknown to Bith, her magic still functioned outside the confines of the iron-bound room, and her spell of protection had cast itself over Brightfeather and all of her friends.

Theirs would be a long and fabled life, the very stuff of sparrow myth. They would frustrate and evade hawk and owl and pestilence throughout their long lifetimes and attain great status among their kind. Evermore, when birds would gather in a tree at sunset to discuss matters both old and new, the story of Brightfeather and her magic flock would grow until, with the passing years, it would take on epic proportions to which others of their kind might only aspire. They would become legend.

CHAPTER
20

Morning had come to the tower before the strange conference was over and all the rats had been briefed on their roles and sent on their appropriate paths. Wallclimber and Blackwhiskers judged that the plan would take the better part of a day to implement.

Furry hordes filtered down the tunnels and cracks and crevices in the tower, down to the dark dungeons below. Once there the rats scurried in through the bars of the windows of the cells, crawling over the apathetic bodies of their inhabitants, easily evading the weak blows and curses that were flung their way.

Sharp teeth began to snick through the wood that held the doors to their hinges. Slowly, the prisoners became aware of the fact that something odd was happening, something most definitely odd. Instead of cursing the rats as was their custom, for they frequently were forced to compete with them for their meager meals, they began to cheer the erstwhile vermin quietly and even offer up bits of food that had been hoarded away against harder times.

The orcs came through the dungeons with buckets, and

the daily gruel was handed out, or rather poured through the narrow openings, and was shared by rats and prisoners alike, a welcome break for the rats, whose mouths were dry and filled with the taste of old wood.

Wallclimber and Blackwhiskers appointed themselves to Endril and Purkins' cell, and their sharp teeth crunched away at the wood, separating it bit by hardened bit from the hinges. All through the morning and afternoon the rats labored, taking care that their efforts were not heard by the orcs, who though not terribly bright, would undoubtedly notice if all the doors to the cells were to fall off their hinges.

For the orc guards morning was a slow time. Aside from the few on duty feeding the prisoners, the rest took the opportunity to sleep late and recover from the previous night's excesses. Their fat, bloated figures snorted and twitched on their lumpy mattresses as they dreamed their orcan dreams and only the cook, his two helpers, and a couple of keymasters stood guard against the equal unlikelihood of an attack or a dungeonbreak.

Two of the slimmest and quickest of the rats had volunteered for the most dangerous job of all. These two slithered into Bebo's quarters and, locating the orc's bed, slipped into his debris-laden pockets, one after the other until they found what they had been searching for, his personal set of knucklebones. Then a judicious bit of gnawing, shaving a bit here and a trifle there, produced the desired effect.

One after the other, the belongings of other sleeping orc guards were similarly attacked by marauding rats until all remaining sets of bones had been found and carefully chewed along various edges. The final result would be that no matter how the knucklebones were rolled, the heretofore unlucky Bebo would always win and his fellow guards would always lose.

· · ·

Unaware of the strange doings in the dungeon, Schlein was still pacing back and forth in his chambers, cursing Tellarko's sloth and berating the deceased scryer, Ormoc, wishing now that he had caused the traitor to suffer longer and more horrible agonies. Death was too easy a fate for such perfidy. Schlein contented contended himself with imagining what he might do to Tellarko if that worthless fool did not return within the hour bearing the necessary ingredient for the healing spell.

After a time, he stopped in front of the mirror and frowned at his visage. Earlier, he had decided that he would not be wed until he was healed. But for reasons of his own, he had decided that today would be the fateful day. Elizebith of Morea would be his, whether she liked it or not. He would enjoy taming her, if she lived through the ordeal. He chuckled, thinking of the girl sitting in chains beside him.

His thoughts returned to Tellarko and he grabbed an hour glass from the shelf. That third-rate magician's time was running out! Schlein turned the glass over and sat down in his chair, waiting for the hour to pass.

Bith was torn between joy and anguish. The tiny note, its few words committed to memory, lay folded against her breast. Cal and the others were coming for her. She had not been forgotten! But how, how could they rescue her? There were just the three of them—maybe four, if that annoying dwarf was still with them—against all of Schlein's evil as well as Murcroft's mischief. The odds were overwhelming.

Despite her former resolve to the contrary, the girl began to hope that Vili would somehow intercede in her behalf. Possibly the god had led her companions off to get the Runesword, spoken of so highly by the dwarf. They would need powerful magic—or an army—to break into this place.

If they didn't rescue her soon then she would be forced to marry Schlein!

"Oh, what to do, what to do!" Back and forth she walked in the confines of her tower cell, hands clasped behind her back, unable to set her mind at rest.

As Bith paced, a slim grey figure slipped in through her window, followed by a second and then a third, brown and piebald in color. Swiftly they crossed the room, keeping to the shadows until they reached the door. Two of them began to scrabble with their claws at the mortar that held the blocks to which the lower hinge was attached. The third climbed the stone blocks to reach the uppermost hinge whereupon it, too, set to work, digging away furiously as though its very life depended on it.

At length the sound of their work penetrated Bith's clouded mind and she turned toward them, frowning as though unable to comprehend what she was seeing.

A shrill scream slipped from her lips as she realized that the door appeared to be swarming with rats. *Rats!* It was all too much! Capture, confinement, Schlein's evil eyes staring at her through the slot in the door, the death of her mystery friend, the loss of her magic, the impending marriage, and now rats! Awful, horrible, disease-ridden rats! Her screams filled the tiny cell and echoed out into the hall past the four orcan guards who now watched her door constantly.

In vain did the rats try to calm Elizebith, in vain did they cluster around her skirts and plead for her attention, in vain did they try to explain who had sent them. But only Blackwhiskers could speak to humans, and he was not there. . . .

Bith placed her hands firmly over her ears and screamed all the more loudly, thinking that she had gone mad or was certainly fast approaching that state. Attacked by a plague of rats!

It could be naught but another ploy of Schlein's. How could he possibly have known that she had a mortal fear of rats? It was the final blow. Hands still clutched to her ears, eyes shut to avoid the sight of little rat paws waving in the air, Bith fell to the floor in a dead, and most unheroic, faint just as the orcan guards unbound the chains that held the iron door fast and pulled on the latch.

The rats did not wait for the door to be unlocked and flung open. They had had ample experience with the orcs and knew all too well the deadliness of orcan knives and crossbows. Many of their friends and relatives had died at orcan hands, and they were not anxious to join those sad numbers. Giving up their efforts to speak to the now unconscious Bith, the rats fled the way they had come. Out the window they went and down the ivy, just as the orcs flung wide the door.

"Is she awright?" asked the largest orc, while another bent over the fallen girl.

"Yeah! Sheez breathin'!" came the answer.

"Must 'uv had a fit or sump'n! C'mon, lets git out uv here, dis room gives me da creeps!" The orcs quickly departed, and the door was again chained and bolted shut.

Tellarko hurried along the dusty road as fast as his aching feet would carry him, cursing the wretch who had stolen his horse, cursing the storekeepers and the housewives who had turned their backs on him and refused to give him the flannel mullein he so desperately required. They would not have dared refuse Schlein or Murcroft, but him, him they refused, looking at him with hatred and turning their backs as though they held him personally responsible for the evil comings and goings associated with the tower and those who dwelt within.

If only he had brought soldiers with him . . . but the wrath of Schlein had rattled him and he had left alone on his quest. One after another, people shut their doors in his face. And then, to cap it all, someone in the last village had stolen his horse, and all of the doors and windows had been bolted against him.

Tellarko headed back toward the tower, certain of his fate when he arrived empty-handed. He had, in fact, almost decided not to return. Then, to his amazement, as though provided by some miracle, there stood a stand of flannel mullein growing by the side of the road, their thick, furry leaves and tall, distinctive, flowering stalks rising above the surrounding underbrush as though willing him to notice.

The flowers thick in their bracts were pink, and Tellarko would have sworn that they should have been gold. They were also covered with a goodly number of bees which swarmed around the flowers and buzzed angrily around his head as he studied the plant. He struggled to remember his basic texts, studied so very long ago, and wondered if there might be a second type of mullein of which he was unaware.

Something, some long-forgotten bit of information was scratching at the door of his memory. It seemed that there was something about those pink flowers. . . . But the thought escaped him, as well it might, for the art of healing was not exactly his forte, nor were his skills that great, for much of his magic consisted of bluff and sleight of hand. Yet one could not do everything. Pink or yellow, it couldn't matter much, could it? Mullein was mullein.

Unwilling to waste any more time pondering the color of flowers, while Schlein was undoubtedly counting grains of sand and thinking up painful ways to do in a lesser magician, Tellarko slapped at the swarming insects and quickly snapped off a dozen of the large furry leaves, tucked them in his pouch and ran off in the direction of the tower, followed by a stream of angry bees.

As he hurried down the road, Tellarko noticed a large number of rats slipping through the fields, flowing across the ruts and streaming through the culverts, all in the direction of Murcroft's tower. Had he not been so concerned about his own well-being, and the number of angry bees that were following him like a long buzzing tail, he might have taken a second look at the odd occurrence. However, his fear of Schlein and his insect pursuers left him no time to worry about strange events in nature.

Tellarko arrived at Schlein's door just as the last grain of sand flowed through the neck of the glass, thus depriving Schlein of the new and ingenious method of torture he had managed to devise for this pudge-faced worm.

"Ah, well, it will keep," Schlein said, chuckling to himself, already in a better mood, knowing that he would use it sooner, rather than later.

"What did you say, my lord?" asked the trembling mage.

"Nothing! Just prepare the potion!"

Fleeing from Schlein's black glance, Tellarko hurried off to his own workroom, pulled a black, leather-bound book from the shelf and opened it to the appropriate page. He ground the flannel mullein into a large silver bowl, carefully following the recipe in the book. He frowned down at the page, for it clearly stated, "two heaping gibbits of *dried* flannel mullein leaves," whereas these were most definitely not dried and were as fresh as fresh could be.

Tellarko hesitated, turning toward the fireplace as though wondering whether he had time to spread and dry the leaves before the fire. Then Schlein's voice echoed through the hall as the evil one bellowed at some other unfortunate servant.

The little man all but swallowed the tip of his beard, which he had been chewing. No, there was no time to dry the leaves; he would just have to make do! Thinking fast,

Tellarko reasoned that dried leaves were bound to be stronger than fresh leaves because fresh leaves took up more space. So, that meant that if he put in three gibbits of fresh leaves . . . no, better make it four gibbits just to be sure . . . the recipe would come out right!

Tellarko sliced, diced, shredded, measured, mixed, boiled, and poured, and at last the mixture was ready and stood steaming in the ceramic cup. But it looked odd . . . definitely odd, something about it was wrong. It was supposed to be bright green, not this ooky shade of brown.

Tellarko frowned at the mixture but it remained the same disgusting color. Then, just as he decided it would be better to face Schlein's wrath rather than deliver a potentially faulty healing potion, the Exalted Master himself stormed into the room, swept the steaming cup out of his hands and swallowed it in a single gulp.

And then, even as the resounding burp echoed through the workroom, Tellarko at last remembered what it was about those pink flowers . . .

"Bee's Burn!" he whispered, snapping his fingers. It had not been flannel mullein at all, but a treacherous relative of the plant called Bee's Burn, so named because of the painful welts it caused upon contact with human flesh. Only the gods could know what would happen to one who swallowed an entire cupful of the stuff!

Tellarko looked down in horror and saw that his hands were turning a bright shade of scarlet and swelling like balloons even as he watched. He glanced up at Schlein, who was holding his belly and emitting yet another enormous belch. He had not yet noticed anything amiss. Tellarko quickly hid his throbbing, swollen hands behind his back, muttered something about a call of nature, and sidled toward the open door.

Schlein waved him away with a laugh. The Exalted Master was in a good mood now and Tellarko seized the moment. He took to his heels and ran. Once his employer realized what he had swallowed . . .

The terrified magician figured he had a few moments of grace to gather up his meager hoard of belongings and get himself gone as far as his most powerful spell would take him. It was written on special scroll he had been saving for many years. A scroll to be used for a quick escape, a scroll that would send him to the farthestmost point in the world. Maybe there he might find a large rock and crawl under it until the distant eon that Schlein would stop looking for him . . . if such a day might ever come.

Tears of fear streamed down Tellarko's ancient cheeks as he fought his way through the rat-clogged halls to his tiny room, praying that he would escape in time. So concerned was he with his own dire straits that he did not even notice the rats.

While Schlein stared into a mirror at his burned body, waiting for the healing process to begin, Endril was watching with satisfaction as Wallclimber and Blackwhiskers chewed through the last shreds of wood that fastened the door to its hinges. The door lurched free with a thump, and Endril caught it and pushed it back in place.

"Just in time," groaned Blackie. "I couldna' swallowed another bite. I may never eat oak again, oooh!"

"Fehh! I know whatcha' mean," Wallclimber said to his companion as he spat a sodden mouthful of chewed wood pulp out of his mouth. "Aged oak is good stuff, but a little bit goes a long way!"

"Our thanks to you, brother rats," said Endril as he wedged bits of wood around the edges of the door so that it did not fall over before they were ready. "We will never forget you."

Blackwhiskers conferred quickly with Wallclimber and the rat leader seemed very agitated, jumping up and down as he squeaked. Finally the talking rat turned to Endril and spoke. "See that you don't," Blackwhiskers replied grimly, fixing the human with a stern eye.

"My word is my bond," Endril said, "whether given to man or rat. You may depend on me."

"And on me," said Purkins, still unaccustomed to speaking to rats. "If I get out of this alive, there will be no more traps or poisoned grain at Purkins Stable. From this day on, you and your kind will be welcome at my hearth."

The two rats bowed to Purkins, and Endril watched the exchange, praying they both would live long enough to honor their pledges, for the doors had been the easiest part of the plan—the hard part was still to come.

Schlein was filled with a curious feeling. He assumed it was happiness, but happiness was not an emotion he was very familiar with, and if he had been asked, he would have said that it felt more like, like, well . . . itching. His burned and blistered skin had not renewed itself as of yet, although the flesh was twitchy and itchy, a sign, he assumed, of healing.

CHAPTER
21

It was like some giant convocation of rats. Wallclimber had sent word by way of the stable rats that any and all available rats in the surrounding countryside were to come to the tower. Hoping, or perhaps guessing, that the summons had something to do with a retaliation against the hated orcs and other assorted villains so recently come to this land, the rats responded in huge numbers. They carpeted the fields, flooded the roads, swarmed over the stiles, and swept toward the tower in a solid stream of chittering, squeaking, squealing rats, all bent on destruction.

Closed up in his tower room, unwilling to see anyone, and totally unaware of the strange activities going on around him, Schlein was just beginning to realize that something was wrong with the potion he had taken. There was still no sign of healing. His skin was an angry, blistery red, what little there was of it, and the flesh beneath was scabrous and ulcerated. But even worse, the itching had grown in its intensity until it was all but unbearable. Everything seemed to itch, both inside and out, and it was all that he could do to keep himself from scratching and tearing at the offending flesh.

His eyelids had swelled nearly shut and it was growing more and more difficult to swallow. In fact, it seemed that his breathing was labored. Growing alarmed, Schlein tottered over to the nearest mirror on feet that felt like wooden lumps with rounded bottoms and peered at himself. What he saw shocked even him. He had swelled to nearly twice his normal size and his features, those same dark features that he so secretly admired, were distorted caricatures spread on a carnival balloon that was his body.

Schlein staggered back and fell into the chair which shuddered beneath his bulk but did not break. He tried to scream out in anger and rage, to scream for Tellarko, who was undoubtedly the cause of his condition, but all that emerged from his swollen mouth, the lips stretched taut over his bared teeth, was a tiny ludicrous squeak!

Time and time again Schlein attempted to call out, but time and again, he failed as his face bulged even larger and his tongue swelled to fill his mouth, scarcely leaving room for a meager trickle of air. Schlein struggled to his feet again and staggered toward the door and help, but halfway across the room he tripped over a small carpet, lost his balance and toppled over onto his back, where he remained as helpless as an overturned turtle.

Consciousness came and went like a flickering candle as Schlein did his best to breathe. Curious half dreams, flashes of the past slid through his mind, himself as a child at his mother's knee. His first spell, turning a cat into a dog, his growing quest for power, and the fatal bargain with the Dark Lord in his turn toward darkness.

Power. Power was everything. He had given up all that was good and noble in the world for the sake of power. His power was vast and he was feared by many. Soon he would own all of the known world.

But for the moment all of his power was for naught. He had been reduced to this foolish spectacle by a wretched girl and the incompetent bunglings of a third-rate magician. With all of his vast power he could not seem to help himself, for his thoughts were scattered and broken by the intermittent loss of consciousness. Schlein clenched his fists and all but wept as the darkness swirled around him and took him down again. If he survived, people would pay, oh, how they would pay . . . but first, he had to survive, and that, he was grimly determined to do.

Tellarko, the unhappy third-rate magician who was responsible for Schlein's ruinous state, had, unfortunately, thus far been unable to remove himself from the tower's confines. His fear of Schlein was great and he wanted nothing more than to be gone, but for some reason his magic scroll would not work. He had recited the words to the teleport spell three times, and each time he had found himself in a different portion of the tower. The first time he had landed in the larder and had assumed that it was but a minor problem, and had used the opportunity to add a haunch of mutton, a bottle of wine and two jars of marmalade to his pack. But the second spell had placed him in Murcroft's parlor, and the third recitation had plunked him in the privy!

Something was dreadfully out of whack and for the life of him—and it *would* be his life, if he didn't solve the problem—he didn't know what to do. Tellarko crept to a tiny closet jammed with broken odds and ends of weapons just outside the door to the orcs' quarters and closed the door behind him, determined to remain there until he got the spell right or night fell and he was able to leave the tower without being seen. He had food. He had drink. He had his spell book. Everything would be all right. Or so he sincerely hoped.

Endril waited impatiently for evening to come, the signal for the lighting of lamps and the beginning of the weekly game of knucklebones.

Tonight was the high point of the guards' dreary existence, for they had been paid their six coppers, less two for room and board. The stakes would be much higher than usual, for due to the increased comings and goings of late, there had been no days of freedom and thus, no opportunity for the orcs to spend their meager funds.

Endril and Purkins crouched in wait behind the door, which was still wedged precariously in place, accompanied by Wallclimber and Blackie as well as numerous other rats who had crept into the cell one by one throughout the long, anxious day. The rats, more impetuous by nature than humans, found it difficult to sit in one place and do nothing and, much to Purkins' discomfort, they crawled up and down the walls and scurried across the floor, their long tails trailing behind them. It was one thing to have their teeth snicking away at the wood door and quite another to have them bared before one's face. Purkins closed his eyes and tried to remember how great a debt they owed the rats, that is, if everything worked according to plan.

In their own due time, the guards cleared the table that stood in the center of the warder room, pulled up the barrels and stools that served as chairs, and brought out the grimy pouches that contained their coins and knucklebones.

The wagering was slow at first and as anticipated, Bebo won. No one was more surprised than Bebo himself but he gladly gathered his winnings to him, chortling with undisguised glee. His comrades were stunned but took his win in stride, telling themselves that it was nothing but a fluke, though grumbling under their breath to let him know their displeasure. Then the bones were cast again and again they marked Bebo as the winner. This time, the grumbles were a good deal louder.

Time and time again the incredulous Bebo won. The knucklebones seemed charmed, incapable of coming up any number but two and seven, the only two numbers that Bebo ever wagered, a fact that was well known to all.

Tempers flared as the pile of coppers rose in front of Bebo. His chortles grew louder and ever more uproarious in direct proportion to his comrades' increasingly black silence. No one other than a simpleton such as Bebo could have failed to notice their growing anger, but so great was his joy that there was little room for anything else in his quite small mind. And even in the best of times, Bebo had not been known for his tact or his sensitivity.

"H, h, hhhey, guys, look, look, look, lookit! I won again!" Bebo stammered, and as he scooped his winnings toward him he noticed that the table was now empty of coins, all save the gleaming mound before him.

"H, h, hhhey, ain't you g, g, gu, guys got no m, m, mmore money?" he asked innocently.

"K, k, k, kin we do this sum m, m, mmore?"

"No we can't do this no more!" snarled Hamhand, the largest and surely the surliest of all the orcs and by far the biggest loser of the evening's game. "You gots all our coppers, bonehead!"

"H, h, hhey, I ain't n, n, nno b, b, bone, bonehead!" Bebo said in an offended tone. "If I was a b, b, b, bone, bonehead I, I wouldna' won, would I of?"

There was little dispute to this logic but it served only to inflame their anger and Fatface, an orc with jowls the size of pumpkins who had also lost every copper he possessed, responded in typical orcan manner by shoving the table forward so that it bumped into Bebo's ample belly.

"Hey, what, what, whatcha' go an', an', an' do that for?" Bebo asked in an aggrieved tone. Without waiting for a reply he shoved the table back, ramming it into Fat-face's own protruding stomach.

The pile of coins slithered across the table and fell onto the floor in a coppery cascade, and all of the orcs immediately scrambled beneath the table and began scooping coppers into their pockets.

"H, h, hhey, quit! Those'er m, m, mmine!" squealed Bebo as he dove into the heaving mass of orcs, pushing them aside none too gently in order to rescue his fortune, perhaps guessing that such a windfall was unlikely to occur again in his lifetime.

"Not yers . . . mine," snorted Hamhand as he thrust a heavy hand into the center of Bebo's chest. "Ya' cheated!"

"D, d, ddid not!" Bebo yelped, rolling across the floor. Closing his own fist, he brought it down on the top of Hamhand's head with a great thump.

"Arrrrrrh!" bellowed Hamhand as he lunged forward and made a grab for Bebo, who made no effort to avoid him but wrapped his arms around Hamhand and rolled him over onto the floor, smashing several other orcs beneath them.

Now, Bebo might not have been the brightest of orcs, even though the words "bright" and "orc" are a contradiction of terms under the best of circumstances, but Bebo was no dummy when it came to fighting, down-and-dirty fighting, the only kind that orcs know.

Knees and fists flashed and curses flew as, one after the other, the entire group of orcs joined in the fight. Coppers scattered in all directions, forgotten, as the orcs threw themselves into the fray, for it had been a long time since they had had a really good fight and there was little that orcs liked better than a really good fight.

As the blood rage settled upon them, clouding what little sense they had and shutting their minds to anything other than the fight at hand, they failed to notice the odd occurrences that began to happen around them.

Tellarko straightened up and held the scroll close to his nose, reading slowly, enunciating each word with great care. This time the spell had to work. He came to the last word and whirled around in a circle three times. There was a whoosh of air and a dizzying moment as the ground went out from under his feet. Then all went silent and he found himself standing in the middle of a room.

The little magician jumped in terror at what he saw laying on the floor at his feet. It was Schlein! He had teleported into the Exalted Master's chamber! His first impulse was to drop everything and run, but then he was struck by an unbelievable sight. His master lay unconscious on the floor . . . but the burned and blistered flesh was healed! Tellarko knelt over Schlein and examined the wounds. Only the slightest of scars, barely visible along his cheek, remained. His eyebrows and lashes had been restored, and even the hairs on the man's barrel chest had returned.

Tellarko rushed to a table and brought a pitcher of water and a cloth and began to dab at his master's face. Schlein stirred, and then his evil yellow eyes came open. Instant rage crossed his brow!

"Why, it's you! You miserable excuse for a . . ." The Exalted Master had his massive hands around his servant's throat, and it was all Tellarko could do to choke out a few words.

"Guk! Urk! No! Wait, Master. Unkh! You are healed. Look in the mirror!"

Schlein dropped Tellarko to the floor like a sack of potatoes, climbed to his feet and walked briskly to the mirror.
His eyes opened wide with amazement, and he ran his hand
through his thick blond hair.

"Well, well. It seems I was a little hasty in my judgment
of your abilities, Tellarko! This is better than I had hoped
for!" Schlein ran his fingers over his huge chin and traced
along the former wounds. "As handsome as ever, wouldn't
you say?"

The little man on the floor sat up and managed to stutter
an answer to his master. He himself could not believe that
the Bee's Burn had produced such a healing effect, yet there
was the proof. Tellarko shook his head and rose to his feet,
hiding his bundle of possessions behind his back.

"Is there aught else that I may do for you, Exalted
Master?"

"Yes!" said Schlein, not taking his eyes off his image
in the mirror. "Go to the kitchen and get the staff ready
for a wedding feast tonight!"

Tellarko crept silently out of the room, relieved that he
had been spared and amazed at the results of his handiwork.
"You clever devil," he mumbled to himself as he descended
the stairs.

One by one the doors to the cells began to fall off their
hinges, and as they fell, out of the openings poured rats;
rats by the hundreds and perhaps even by the thousands
cascading into the warder room. There were prisoners as
well, among the furry mass, wizened and pale prisoners
staggering around and shading their eyes against the unexpected brightness of the torch-lit room, uncertain what to
do with their newfound freedom and more than a little be-
mused by the role of the rats.

But Endril and Purkins had no such doubts. Both of them

seized sturdy lengths of firewood and fell upon the mound of heaving, cursing orcs, adding their own blows to those the orcs were inflicting upon each other. Given a direction, it did not take the other prisoners long to follow suit. Long years of animosity, long years of suffering, long years of rage boiled over as the prisoners gave vent to their feelings.

The startled orcs, only just realizing that something was wrong, found themselves besieged by their prisoners, who were no longer behind locked doors but free in the warder room, wielding sticks and chairs and in a few cases the orcs' own weapons.

The orcs tried to fight back, but it was too late, for the prisoners were aided by what seemed like all the rats in the world, who climbed the orcs' leather armor with ease and bit at every inch of exposed flesh, swarming over them, burying them beneath mounds of fur and lashing tails and sharp, flashing teeth. And had Endril not called them off, there was little doubt that the rats would have killed them all in short order.

As it was, the rats were not pleased. "Why'dja call us off?" whistled Blackwhiskers. "Dja know how many of us they kill alla' time? They calls it rabbick schtew, but it was really us and not no rabbicks at all."

Endril felt his stomach heave, but he fought his nausea down. "Leave them to us for the time being, Master Rat, and you shall decide their fate in the end. We may yet need them as bargaining chips before we win our freedom from this evil place."

The orcs were not making matters any easier, for as they were being bound and chained they cursed their captors and heaped insults on their parentage and that of the rats as well, not knowing when it was best to hold their tongues.

Wallclimber had difficulty controlling his followers, for many of their friends and relatives had found their way into the orcan stewpots over the years and they were more than ready for revenge. But in the end, Blackwhiskers and Endril prevailed. There was plenty of grain and food to be divided up, and that would keep the rat pack busy for days while the humans dealt with the orcs.

Lifting the ring of keys from Hamhand's belt, Endril turned to the crowd and cried, "Now! To the tower to rescue my lady!"

"To the tower!" echoed the crowd of prisoners, who had by now armed themselves with orcan blades and polearms. The dungeon door flew open and out poured a torrent of angry men and a scurrying sea of rats. Through the tortuous winding passageways they climbed, overwhelming unsuspecting guards at each post, and releasing other prisoners from their cells. The swelling army finally burst through into the lowest level of the tower and subdued the human guards at the armory. Endril took more keys and opened it up. Additional weapons were passed out, and Endril was especially pleased to find his magic glove and special sword hanging on the wall. He reclaimed his old weapons and then led his strange army of rats and men out again and up the tower stairs in search of Bith.

The noise of the escaping prisoners, plus the pitter-pat of some several thousands of rat footsteps thundering up the stairs, roused Schlein from his dreams of grandeur and he made his way to the door. He peeked out into the passageway just in time to see the onrushing crowd of angry men and rats.

"Hellfire and brimstone!" he exclaimed, and slammed the door quickly shut, throwing the bolt as well. He lumbered across the room to a secret panel and disappeared into the wall.

• • •

Tellarko had barely finished his instructions to the cook when there was a great disturbance in the next room. The doors to the kitchen flew open and in poured a swarm of rats followed by the angriest bunch of bearded men he had ever seen. And they were all brandishing big swords! Needing no encouragement, the magician and the chef dropped what they were doing and hightailed it out the back door, through the back gate, and into the woods.

Bith had regained consciousness, but was unable to summon the strength or the will to rise. She lay on the old flagstones and watched as the sun slowly fell from its zenith and wondered who would come for her first. Schlein, Cal . . . or the rats.

Suddenly, the sounds of conflict filled the stairway and then the thunder of an advancing horde. The orcan guards were overwhelmed and Endril seized the key ring and attacked the lock. The door was flung open, crashing against the far wall, and Endril and Purkins and hundreds of rats poured into the room. Bith screamed, thinking Endril to be no more than some illusion sent by Schlein to torture her. She believed in the awful reality of the rats, however, who rummaged among her skirts and crawled over her arms and legs, snicking and chittering in cruel imitation of speech while their long, naked tails dragged across her skin.

The false image of Endril along with the undeniable reality of hundreds of rats was too much for Bith and she buried her face in her hands and sobbed.

"What's this, Elizebith, are you not pleased to see me?" asked the illusion that was Endril. "Or have you developed a liking for Schlein's company in my absence?" The false image mocked her mischievously.

"Oh, don't, don't tease me so. It is too cruel," sniffed

Bith. "Endril, Endril, if only you were really here. I cannot bear it any longer. I wish I were dead."

The elf knelt before the girl and took her hand gently in his. "Bith, dear friend, do not weep. I did not mean to tease you. Come, will you not look into my face? I am really here. We have come to your rescue. These rats are my friends and you are saved. Come away now, let us leave this place, quickly."

Bith looked into Endril's eyes, her face streaked with the passage of tears which clung to her lashes like drops of crystalline dew, and saw that it truly was Endril kneeling there before her. Ignoring the rats, who unfortunately were still there as well, she gazed on Endril's face with longing and touched his cheek with her fingers.

"Oh, Endril. It *is* you!" she cried, flinging her arms around his neck. "How is this possible?"

"It is a long and complicated story and best saved for another day," said Endril as he gathered Bith's slender form into his arms and carried her through the door. "But I could not have done it by myself. This is John Purkins here beside me, but it is these fine rats we have to thank for our freedom. We owe them all."

"Rats," Elizebith echoed weakly, somewhat astonished to discover that she owed her freedom to a pack of rats, rats, whom she had always feared and despised. A tremulous smile flitted across her lips and she found it returned a hundred fold by the long-tailed, sharp-toothed hairy horde who frolicked squeaking at Endril's feet as they made their way down the stairs to freedom.

Rats, prisoners, orcs, and Endril and Bith opened the final door and streamed into the cobblestone courtyard where they milled around in joyful confusion, wondering what to do next.

Several human guards stood staring at them in amazement, and as the prisoners advanced on them with swords clutched firmly in their hands, the guards threw down their own weapons and took to their heels, fleeing before the determined crowd.

Rats and humans alike let out a great cheer, for it seemed that the last obstacle had been defeated. Now nothing lay between them and freedom.

Purkins and a group of former prisoners ran off to the stables and returned shortly with all of the horses, saddled and ready to ride. Presenting the reins of a fine bay gelding and a roan mare to Endril, the smith bowed low before the pair, suddenly shy in their presence.

"Myself and the others, we thank you for what you have done this day. I hope you find the rest of your friends and finish doing what you set out to do. Come back and see us sometime, if you can. You'll always have friends in this part of the world." The smith's words were met with the cheers and good wishes of the other prisoners and those of the rats as well.

Bith mounted the gelding and smiled broadly. Endril climbed into the saddle beside her and they turned their horses toward the gate.

CHAPTER
22

Greybeard finished the tale of the king's bottomless well just as the three came to the top of a small rise, overlooking Murcroft's tower. It was night, but the waxing moon cast its light on the valley before them. Cal was hungry, and now that the spell of the dwarf was gone, his legs ached and wanted rest. But that was not to be. There before them was a crowd of horsemen riding along the road that wound through the forest to the tower gate. Gunnar, who must have seen more with his keen eyesight jumped up and down excitedly.

"No time to lose! Grab my sleeve and stay by my side!"

At once, Cal, Hathor, and the dwarf broke into a wild run, as they had done once before when escaping from the black dragon. The trees whirled past in a blur as the trio sped through the night, heading for the tower.

The guards at the gate, who had not yet been subdued by the army of rats and freed prisoners, suddenly appeared along the battlements, armed with crossbows. At the same time, the sound of thundering hooves came over the walls.

Then the main gate swung open and a hundred armored horsemen, with Murcroft in the lead, stormed in. Brandishing their swords, they fell upon the stunned, disorganized rabble that milled about in the courtyard.

Hundreds of hapless rats were trampled underfoot and countless others scampered away in all directions. Arrows and bolts flew through the air, felling several of the prisoners. Bith's mount reared in terror and she was thrown to the ground. Purkins managed to pull her to safety as several of Murcroft's horsemen rode through their midst.

Endril drew his sword and tried to rally a group of prisoners, but they had dropped their weapons and fled into the shadowy shelter of the walls. The elf lashed out at a pair of soldiers who fell upon him and swept their swords from their hands. The horsemen retreated out of the reach of his sword and formed a circle around those few defenders who stood in the center of the courtyard. An uneasy silence fell over the scene, broken only by the snorting horses and the moans of the wounded.

Purkins, Bith, and Endril were surrounded. The elf put his arm around the girl and held his sword defiantly. Bith fumbled in her belt, aware for the first time that her magic abilities had returned. From above, great rhythmic blasts of wind blew clouds of dust in every direction, and the horses grew restless and backed away.

Endril glanced up, and jerked Purkins and Bith out of the way as the huge claws of the black dragon thumped into the earth. As the enormous creature settled among the frightened horsemen and terrified prisoners in the courtyard, Schlein, who sat on a golden saddle on the monster's shoulders, began to laugh.

"Well, I have to hand it to you, Elizebith," snarled the Exalted Master. "You have caused me more trouble than I could have imagined possible."

The dragon's ugly claw snaked slowly up to the evil man and Schlein climbed out of the saddle and into the monster's grasp.

"Tonight was to have been our wedding night! Such a shame, for I fear that will no longer be possible!"

The dragon placed Schlein on the ground.

"I can no longer be bothered with all the trouble you and your friends stir up. By midnight the stake will be ready and the witch of Baoancaster will burn!" He mashed his fist into his palm and then turned to Murcroft. "Prepare the pyre!" Schlein then glanced into the shadows behind the ring of horsemen at the cowering prisoners and the few remaining visible rats. "And see that none of these *vermin* live!"

Guards closed in on Bith, Endril, and Purkins, and mounted soldiers turned their horses to follow Schlein's orders.

Suddenly, out of the night, a great horn sounded, a horrific blast of piercing sound that made the very earth shake. The horses shied in panic, throwing their riders, and began stampeding about, throwing the courtyard into a riot of confusion. The thick, iron-bound gates of the tower broke loose from the stones that flanked it and came tumbling down, crushing the unfortunate guards underneath.

Endril and Purkins grabbed Bith and hurried her back to the tower stair. Schlein bellowed a series of oaths and then beat one horse after another to the ground with his fists, fighting his way toward Elizebith.

"Endril, look!" the girl squealed, pointing at the gate. There, standing in the gateway were Cal, Hathor, and the dwarf. The young warrior held a glowing blade above his head. Schlein turned and saw this too, then commanded the black dragon.

"Destroy them, *now*!"

A few soldiers staggered to their feet and charged the newcomers, but Caltus was too fast for them and leaped to first one side and then the other in a blur of speed. Hathor swung wide with his axe, lopping the heads off three of them, and the rest quickly fell back in fear. The boy walked defiantly out into the center of the courtyard, holding the shield in one hand and Sjonbrand in the other. The sword was glowing blue green and hummed ominously like a thousand angry bees.

The black dragon whirled around in its slow, methodical fashion and fixed its eyes on the boy. Hathor, meanwhile, was making his way around the courtyard, hacking and slashing at any soldier unfortunate enough to get in his way, and the dwarf followed quietly in the troll's wake. With a great rumble the dragon puffed up its huge black chest and let out a scorching blast of flame that rolled across the courtyard, totally engulfing Cal.

A cry of amazement went up from those present, and Bith screamed. As the flames subsided and the black smoke drifted clear, Cal emerged, unharmed. His helm and shield, and the bracelets and the horn of gold, however, had melted away. His clothing too, had disintegrated. The boy stood naked, grasping the humming Sjonbrand with both hands.

Caltus let out a wild battle cry and lunged at his opponent. Before the dragon could react, the sword plunged deep into the beast's breast. The black monster let out an agonizing wail and crashed slowly to the ground at the boy's feet.

Schlein uttered another oath and began a furious motioning with his hands. An orange aura appeared around his body and then he disappeared in a cloud of white smoke. Murcroft, seeing how things were going, melted away into the darkness, and the prisoners and rats once again sprang forth ready to do battle.

But the fight was gone from the defenders of the tower

and with Schlein and Murcroft gone, they quickly surrendered. The rats and former prisoners returned to carry off their dead and wounded.

Soon the courtyard was deserted, save the four outcasts: Cal, Hathor, Endril, and Bith, united again.

Endril lead Bith down the stairs and they joined their friends beside the body of the slain dragon. Bith giggled at Cal, and the boy, suddenly aware of his nakedness, turned red as a beet, grabbed Hathor's bearskin cape and threw it around his body. The dwarf appeared out of the darkness and began jumping up and down with joy.

"This is wonderful, you have slain the black dragon . . . Schlein and Murcroft have run away! Hoo ha! The Dark Lord is not going to like this!"

Bith apologized to her friends for thinking that they had deserted her. Cal smiled.

"This time we have done well. I may have lost my golden helm and shield, but we still have Sjonbrand the Skryling's blade!" With a grunt, he pulled the weapon out of the dragon's breast and held it aloft with one hand.

To the horror of all, the sword began to melt, and drizzled away drop by drop as though it were water.

"Not again!" screamed Cal.

"I'm sure Vili is behind all this!" Endril remarked dourly.

Without warning, the usually quiet Hathor grabbed the dwarf by the scruff of his neck and held him up off the ground.

"Just who is your master?"

The dwarf choked out the word, "Vili! But I was under an oath, I could not tell you . . . not until now."

Hathor dropped him to the ground, slapping his big paw to his forehead.

"Well you have to admit that you're safe and sound

now," said the dwarf, rubbing his small hands together, "and all thanks to Vili and Sjonbrand. It really was forged by my own hand, you know. It pains me, as well, to see it destroyed, though I knew it must be done!"

"What about our reward?" demanded Bith. "I went through living hell so you could destroy that damned sword."

"Well, I . . ." Greybeard fumbled in his pack and produced a bag of gold. Bith snatched it angrily.

"Oh no!" the dwarf cried sadly. Out of his pack came the broken remains of the endless bottle of wine. "I'm sorry, Hathor, it must have broken during the battle."

"Ooo, now I really need a drink!" exclaimed the troll.

"You're not alone!" chimed in Cal.

The dwarf produced another sack of gold from inside his shirt and held it up.

"This, my friends, is the end of my fortune, really! Here, take it!" Endril took the purse and tied it to his belt. The dwarf continued, "Now, as I recall from my explorations, Murcroft had quite a wine cellar in yon tower. It is ours for the taking. Ha! How fitting. The drinks are on Murcroft!" He glanced up at the moon. "I have time for a few, then I must return post haste to Northunderland. A matter of a certain borrowed ship that must be returned!"

Endril and Bith said nothing, and the five of them walked slowly back up the steps and into the tower, where they were joined by Purkins, the rats, and the others who had helped them defeat Schlein and his minions. The celebration that followed became part of the legend.